THE

Robert Bloch was born in 1917
and Stella Loeb, both of German J
attended a screening of the Lon Cha
the scene where Chaney removes his mask terrified the young Bloch and sparked an early interest in horror. A precocious child, he was already in the fourth grade at age eight and obtained a pass for the adult section of the library, where he was a voracious reader. At age ten, in 1927, Bloch discovered *Weird Tales* and became an avid fan, with H.P. Lovecraft, a frequent contributor to the magazine, becoming one of his favorite writers. In 1933 Bloch began a correspondence with Lovecraft, which would continue until the older writer's death in 1937. Bloch's early work would be heavily influenced by Lovecraft, and Lovecraft offered encouragement to the young writer.

Bloch's first short story was published in 1934 and would be followed by hundreds of others, many of them published in *Weird Tales*. His first collection of tales, *The Opener of the Way* (1945) was issued by August Derleth's Arkham House, joining an impressive list of horror writers that included Lovecraft, Derleth, Clark Ashton Smith, and Carl Jacobi. His first novel, *The Scarf*, would follow two years later, in 1947. He went on to publish numerous story collections and over thirty novels, of which the most famous is *Psycho* (1959), the basis for Alfred Hitchcock's classic film. He won the prestigious Hugo Award (for his story "The Hell-Bound Train") as well as the Bram Stoker Award and the World Fantasy Award. His work has been extensively adapted for film, television, radio, and comics. He died of cancer at age 77 in 1994.

Also Available by Robert Bloch

The Opener of the Way
Pleasant Dreams
Strange Eons
The Night of the Ripper
Midnight Pleasures

ROBERT BLOCH

THE SCARF

With a new introduction by
GARYN G. ROBERTS

VALANCOURT BOOKS

Author's Note: Any resemblance to actual incidents or to persons living or dead—including the author—is purely coincidental.

The Scarf by Robert Bloch
Originally published by The Dial Press in 1947
First Valancourt Books edition 2025

Published by Valancourt Books, Richmond, Virginia
http://www.valancourtbooks.com

ISBN 978-1-960241-43-6 (trade hardcover)
ISBN 978-1-960241-42-9 (trade paperback)
Also available as an electronic book.

Set in Dante MT

INTRODUCTION

Robert Bloch, my friend, was dying in the late, hot months of the summer of 1994.

I never met Robert Bloch in person, but we had been voracious and prolific correspondents since the mid-1980s. Mr. Bloch had read some of my published work, and he liked these pieces. He was enthusiastically supportive of me writing and publishing more about his life and times.

He told me that we needed to hurry.

The doctors hoped he would see Christmas. The cancer had metastasized to more than one organ; they could combat some of it, but not all.

Mr. Bloch (77) was in Los Angeles; I (35) was moving from East Lansing to Traverse City, Michigan.

Though I sent him pages of questions to answer, and a tape recorder, by mid-summer '94, his voice was dramatically failing, and though he tried valiantly, we were past a time to use the recorder. He wrote long letters and postcards almost daily, and answered my questions as best he could.

Things happened very quickly that September.

Only a few days before he was gone, Mr. Bloch wrote me a postcard saying "Good-Bye." Physicians were making him comfortable. He was fading and would have to end our correspondence.

Never losing his sense of humor and sense of irony, he signed this last postcard, "Oncologically, Bob." Tears ran down my face.

Christmas never arrived for Mr. Bloch in 1994. He passed September 23rd of that year. It is said that Bloch was very upset when Lovecraft passed, maybe in some small way my distress was similar.

Robert Albert Bloch was born in the greater Chicago area

to Raphael Ray Bloch (1884-1952) and Stella Loeb (1880-1944) in 1917. One night in 1925, the year the movie debuted, he went to a late-night screening of Lon Chaney's silent classic, *The Phantom of the Opera*. That same year, he saw the movie *The Lost World*, a Professor Challenger adventure based on the legendary Arthur Conan Doyle (1859-1930) series.

In 1929, the Bloch family moved north to Milwaukee. Still in his childhood, Bloch discovered and devoured the then Chicago-based pulp magazine, *Weird Tales*. But his literary consumption was not limited to what would become the most important dark fantasy and imagination-based periodical of all time. The teen-aged Bloch read science fiction, fantasy, adventure, and detective fiction pulps. He started contributing to and becoming involved with science fiction fanzines and fandom, and by 1935 joined The Milwaukee Fictioneers, a writing group that included Stanley G(rauman) Weinbaum (1902-35), Ralph Milne Farley (pseudonym for Roger Sherman Hoar, 1887-1963), and Raymond A(rthur) Palmer (1910-77).

As early as 1933, Robert Bloch began correspondence with H(oward) P(hillips) Lovecraft (1890-1937). The story of Lovecraft and Bloch's ongoing correspondence, and their tributes paid to each other in their stories—stories they both published in *Weird Tales*—is legendary. Bloch appears as the character "Robert Blake" in the Lovecraft story "The Haunter of the Dark" (*Weird Tales*, December 1936). Lovecraft dedicated this story to Bloch—it was the only time the master dedicated a story to a single person. Between 1935 and 1952, Bloch had sixty-seven short stories, novellas, and novelettes appear in *Weird Tales* alone. In the 1930s and '40s, he also had stories of various lengths and types published in a range of other magazines, including, but not limited to, *Amazing Stories*, *Fantastic Adventures*, *Imaginative Tales*, *Strange Stories*, *Unknown Worlds* and *Unusual Stories*.

"The Secret in the Observatory," *Amazing Stories* (August 1938), a novella, was Robert Bloch's first published "science fiction" story. It was the cover story of that issue. Bloch's first hard-cover book was his collection of short stories (many from *Weird Tales*), published by August Derleth's Arkham House of Sauk City, Wisconsin. This was entitled *The Opener of the Way* (1945).

While Bloch had many successful and memorable stories published in the '30s, '40s and '50s, three of particular note are "The Cheaters" (*Weird Tales*, November 1947), "Catnip" (*Weird Tales*, March 1948) and "That Hell-Bound Train" (*The Magazine of Fantasy and Science Fiction*, September 1958). There are so many good ones, published in a range of genres and places.

Like Bloch's 1947 novel *The Scarf*, the storyline of "The Cheaters" is organized episodically. "The Cheaters" is a novelette, or long short story, which traces the movements of a pair of eyeglasses or spectacles through the lives of the people who possess the ocular instruments. The cheaters provide their users with horrific and maddening insights into the supernatural and a darker world. Classic Bloch wordplay is in place, and the interconnected episodes of the story lead to an effective and satisfying conclusion. It was adapted for Boris Karloff's *Thriller* television series (December 27, 1960).

"Catnip" is a nasty little story about a nasty, not-so-little, juvenile delinquent boy named Ronnie Shires. Ronnie is a bully who torments an elderly neighbor lady. By careless accident, Ronnie starts the old lady's home on fire with his cigarette. Yet vengeance comes in the form of the old lady's cat, and hence the title of the story takes on significance as pun and black humor.

Though not exactly, "That Hell-Bound Train" is a wonderful Faustian "Deal with the Devil" pact-type story. Twists and turns and time travel mark this tale. First published in 1958, it earned the Hugo Award (science fiction's prestigious fan award) for best short story in 1959.

One of Bloch's early *Weird Tales* was the now legendary "Yours Truly, Jack the Ripper" (July 1943); this story has been repeatedly adapted for radio, television, and comic books. It appeared on radio as an episode for *Stay Tuned for Terror*. In 1944, Bloch was asked to adapt *Weird Tales* stories into radio episodes for this radio series. The program was advertised in the pages of *Weird Tales* magazine. Many (if not all) of the episodes were adaptations of the author's own *Weird Tales* stories. Sadly, only two episodes are known to exist today, making installments of *Stay Tuned for Terror* some of the most elusive, mythical and sought-after pieces of radio drama history ever. These two episodes are based upon

Robert Bloch's "The Bogeyman Will Get You" (*Weird Tales*, March 1946) and "Lizzie Borden Took an Axe" (*Weird Tales*, May 1947). Bloch's "Almost Human" (*Fantastic Adventures*, July 1943), a science fiction tale, appeared as a radio drama first on NBC's *Dimension X* (May 13, 1950) and then later on that same network's *X Minus One* (August 11, 1955).

Robert Bloch's list of movie credits is impressive and extensive. These began in the early 1960s when the author moved to Hollywood upon the success of *Psycho* (1959 novel; 1960 Alfred Hitchcock motion picture). Similarly impressive and extensive is Robert Bloch's list of television credits, including three of the best episodes of the original *Star Trek*—"What Are Little Girls Made Of" (October 20, 1966), "Catspaw" (October 27, 1967), and "Wolf in the Fold" (December 22, 1967).

In terms of bio-bibliography, story context and analysis, and related chronicling the life and works of Robert Bloch, two works sit atop all the rest. These are Randall D. Larson's books for Starmont House, and Robert Bloch's *Once Around the Bloch: An Unauthorized Autobiography* (New York: Tor, 1993). Bloch's autobiography is an absolute gem on many levels.

Robert Bloch's *The Scarf* was first published in 1947 by Dial Press of New York. This hardcover was Bloch's first professionally published novel and only his second book. The first edition of *The Scarf* was printed on very poor-quality paper stock, and the rare copies remaining today feature very brown, brittle acid-ridden pulp paper. Consequently, copies of that first edition are invariably in rough condition today. For decades the works of Robert Bloch have been some of the most sought-after, and some of the most difficult to find, in collectible bookshops.

A range of paperback reprints followed in the next two decades, and each of these featured alluring, beautiful cover art. The 1966 Gold Medal paperback of *The Scarf* featured some story revisions and updates.

Robert Bloch was still in his twenties when he wrote this novel. The story is told in first-person narration from the perspective of a struggling novelist named Dan Morley. Is *The Scarf* a highly exaggerated memoir recounting some of Robert Bloch's own trials and tribulations in the publishing business? On the copyright page, Bloch provides the following disclaimer: "Any resemblance to actual incidents or to persons living or dead—including the author—is purely coincidental."

Published twelve years before *Psycho*, *The Scarf* is organized episodically. It begins in the Midwest (Minneapolis and then Chicago) and eventually moves to New York and Hollywood.

While it is a book that very effectively stands on its own, *The Scarf* is a psychological thriller that could very much be considered a prequel to, an early run at themes Bloch further developed in *Psycho*. Themes of psychology, including references to Freud, maternal figures, coming-of-age angst, and sex are all interwoven into Bloch's tale. There is a noirish quality to the atmosphere, and interspersed dark humor.

The scarf itself is a deadly icon whose use is a motif. The first chapter with Miss Frazer (38) and Dan (18) is intense, and the rest of the novel follows a well-organized and articulated train wreck. To offset the very dark atmospheres and themes of his stories, Bloch often incorporated levity and some of the best dark comedy ever found in the dark fantasy and thriller genres. Some of this comedy is dependent upon coincidence, fate that is the product of the bad behavior of story characters, and on wordplay.

For better or worse, Bloch knew that he would always be best remembered as the man who wrote the novel that Alfred Hitchcock made into the movie *Psycho*. He had mixed feelings about this since he already had many hundreds of successful short stories, radio dramas, television plays, movie scripts, and more of which he was justifiably proud. Robert Bloch was a writer's writer, and he was quiet and humble. He was unassuming and literally had a wicked sense of humor. He was the master of the twist ending, and this led readers to compare his work to that of O. Henry (William Sydney Porter, 1862-1910). In his vast correspondence to the author of this introduction, Bloch included the following:

> All I ever acquired were the simple tricks of my trade—the ability to play games with words. This is only enough to provide me with a half-life, hidden away in the pages of books

which are in turn hidden away on bookshelves here and there, now and for a little while in the immediate future. After that there'll be nothing; the memories of those who knew me will fade, and my name will be referred to in passing only by those researching the "pop culture" of this soon-to-vanish century."[1]

No twentieth-century author was more loved than Robert Bloch. Though underappreciated in his time, many of us love him to this day. More than a very talented writer, Robert Bloch was a good man, mentor, and dear friend.

My sincere thanks go to the fine, visioned people—my new-found friends—at Valancourt. And to my brother Bob Craig who apprised me of the upcoming Robert Bloch book series from Valancourt.

GARYN G. ROBERTS
Arbor Vitae, Wisconsin
August 22, 2024

Garyn G. Roberts, Ph.D., is a college and university professor. His book, *Dick Tracy and American Culture*, was an Edgar Award Finalist; his *The Prentice Hall Anthology of Science Fiction and Fantasy* won the Popular Culture Association's Ray and Pat Browne Book of the Year Award. Roberts has also recently written introductions for three volumes of Edgar Rice Burroughs' Centennial and Definitive Editions. His lifelong interests include the life and works of Chester Gould, and Robert Bloch, and his dear friend, Ray Bradbury. Further passions include nineteenth- and twentieth-century popular fiction, newspaper comic strips, dime novels and pulp magazines, science fiction and fantasy, and mystery and detective fiction. After many years of collecting and writing, Dr. Roberts is coming closer to completing his extensive book-length tribute to Robert Bloch—a project Bloch himself helped with before his passing in 1994.

1 From Robert Bloch, "Unpublished Introduction" for upcoming book by Garyn G. Roberts. Introduction dated July 26, 1994, two months before Robert Bloch's death.

This book is for
MARION AND SALLY ANN

GENESIS

Fetish? You name it. All I know is, I've had to have it with me. Ever since I was a kid back at Horton High, I had to have it. Ever since. . . .

Lying on the bed, looking at the scarf, I spilled everything:

I had this Miss Frazer for a teacher in Senior English, and she fell in love with me.

It's easy to say it now, but at the time I didn't even realize what was happening. I couldn't think of such a thing then without blushing.

Yes, I was pretty naïve at that: bookish, full of ideals and adolescent nonsense. She did her part to help it along by criticizing my themes and encouraging me to write stories and poetry.

That's a laugh, isn't it? Me, writing poetry. Staying after school and letting Miss Frazer help me scan *Idylls of the King.* I can still remember how cold it would get, those late winter afternoons in the empty classroom, the air bitter with the smell of chalk-dust.

Miss Frazer was just a spinster school teacher, and I was teacher's pet. As far as I was concerned that was our relationship, and it satisfied me. She made no demands, she was only an understanding friend. I didn't realize it at the time, but what she really offered me was a womb to crawl into when I felt low. A spinster's womb—safe, sterile, sexless. Antisocial, antiseptic, antiphysical.

But I didn't know what was going on in Miss Frazer's mind. I couldn't have imagined the possibility. Why, she must have been thirty-eight, her hair was turning gray, and she wore horn-rimmed glasses. I was eighteen.

She called me Daniel. She talked to me about my future, about going to college. About the worship of beauty. About kindred spirits dedicated to the sacred flame. And she would take off her glasses and look at me while I read aloud to her.

I didn't suspect what was wrong with her. Frustrated, I guess you'd call it. She was sincere, all right. Perhaps that was the real trouble—she was too sincere. She believed what she was saying. About how two souls can be attuned.

But I didn't understand. The kids razzed me about it, even my folks razzed me. I didn't care, because I believed in Miss Frazer. When she started asking me to drop in evenings at her house, I went.

That was all right. My folks knew about it. She was a churchgoer, respectable. She reminded me a lot of my mother—only she was nicer, kinder, more understanding. My mother was——

But never mind that, now. The important thing is, I went to visit Miss Frazer once or twice a week, regularly, and nothing out of the way ever happened. Sometimes she put her hand on my shoulder when we read together, that's all.

Nothing happened for almost a year, and then everything happened at once.

One Saturday night, just before graduation, I went up to her place with a short story she wanted me to send to *Story* magazine. Somehow we got to talking about graduation coming and me going away to college.

I remember she was all dressed up as if it was Sunday, and that made me notice her for the first time as a woman. As a female, that is.

I guess it hit me after she began to cry. Because suddenly, right in the middle of a sentence, she burst out crying. Not burst out, exactly. She just sobbed, very quietly.

Naturally, I felt embarrassed. I asked her what was the matter.

She told me. Told me she couldn't stand the thought of these evenings coming to an end and me going away. She had led a terrible life, this meant so much to her, and now even these little crumbs would be gone.

I still didn't catch on. I guess she knew that and tried to cover up. All at once she became very gay. She asked me if I would like some wine.

By this time I was so flustered, I didn't know how to act or what to say. Believe it or not, I'd never taken a drink in my life. The very idea of a school teacher taking a drink shocked me.

But I said yes, and we had some wine. Muscatel, I guess it was.

She kept talking a mile a minute to distract me, asking me to please excuse an old woman for her weakness; apologizing for being so silly and sentimental.

We had some more wine, and I began to get dizzy. It was hot in there; the night was fairly cool and she'd turned the gas-log way up. I felt flushed and everything was out of focus.

She sat next to me on the sofa, staring at me until I squirmed. Then she said she had a present for me. Something she'd made—a sort of graduation gift.

And she brought out the scarf. The maroon scarf.

I thanked her. I'll never forget the look on her face. She asked me if I'd mind expressing my thanks to her—she could scarcely bring herself to say it—by kissing her.

I swear it didn't sound silly, then. It wasn't silly. It was desperate. Everything; her voice, her expression, the heat, the wine, the tension. Desperate.

I kissed her. She was thirty-eight, her hair was graying, she was a small-town school teacher, an old maid.

But she put her arms around me and came close. I closed my lips tight as a trap, but I could feel her hot, slick tongue pulsing against them.

I don't know what happened after that, if anything happened. Anything could have, because I passed out. The heat, the wine, the excitement did the trick.

Finally I came to. She had pulled down all the blinds. The lights were out, and not even the gas-log glowed. It was utterly black in there.

I was still lying on the sofa, but something had happened to my hands. They were bound together—by the maroon scarf.

For a minute I was too scared to move. Then I heard a noise, two noises. The first noise was a gasping; Miss Frazer was lying on the floor beside me, wheezing and sobbing. The second noise was a hissing.

She had turned the unlit gas-log up, full on.

I could smell it now, the odor filled the room. My head throbbed from the wine, and from the gas that was flooding the darkness.

"Miss Frazer!" I yelled.

She wouldn't listen. She held me down on the sofa, while she had hysterics. We were damned, doomed, lost. We could never face the world. We had betrayed Beauty. Now we must pay for it. And at least we could die together. We were going to sacrifice ourselves to Beauty.

I tried to fight her off. She clung to me, and the odor seeped up all around us, seeped into us.

I remember exactly how it felt. The darkness began to change, explode. Hundreds of red dots wavered and swam before my eyes. They turned to circles, whirling circles of fire. Far away I could hear her voice, panting out about Death and Resurrection.

Then even the voice faded off, and there was only the panting. It got deep, horribly deep. I wanted to close my eyes against the circles, close my ears to that hideous rasping of her breath.

Somehow I squirmed out from under her and off the sofa, my arms tied behind me. I managed to stand up, swaying back and forth. She was somewhere below me, but I couldn't see her. I tried to yell at her to open the windows, untie my hands. She didn't hear. I couldn't hear my own voice. The hissing circles swam away from me. I began to stumble across the room. It took years. I bent my head and began to run through the darkness. I ran forever. Then I crashed headlong into the window.

The window smashed. I hung halfway out of it, in a tangle of splintered glass, retching as the air hit my lungs. Then I passed out again.

When they found us, I was still hanging there. And Miss Frazer was unconscious. I suppose enough air came in around me to keep her alive.

I won't repeat what they said when they found us like that, or what she said. They took us both to the hospital, and it was pretty bad. The day after I was released, I ran away. I had to run away—I couldn't stand it. For years I hated women, books, everything.

But somehow, I always kept that scarf.

MINNEAPOLIS

I

When I pushed open the door Rena was lying on the sofa, pretty as a picture—if you like that sort of picture.

She had her hair done in an upsweep, and she was wearing a pair of blue pajamas. She was finishing a cigarette and getting ready to add it to the pile of red-tipped butts crushed in the ash tray next to the sofa.

I didn't need to look twice to see that she was slightly drunk.

"Hello, Rena," I said.

She sat up and put down her glass.

"Darling—let me look at you!"

It was a reasonable request.

I put down my overnight bag and pirouetted around the room like a swish, giving her an eyeful of my new brown double-breasted suit, tan shirt, green tie and brown military pumps.

It was the least I could do. After all, she'd paid for them.

"Like it?" I said, putting a hand on my hip.

"Love it," said Rena. She giggled. "Quit clowning, will you?" She held out her arms.

I went over and kissed her. She was drunk, all right.

"Hey, wait a minute," I said, pulling away. "Want to wrinkle my new suit?"

"Uh-huh."

She started to reach under the sofa for the bottle and then she saw the overnight bag on the floor.

"Darling, you're moving in?"

She jumped up and threw her arms around me. I tried to head her off, but she babbled so fast I couldn't get a word in edgeways.

"Now that you're getting out of that flophouse you can stay here days while I'm working and finish your story, and we'll——"

"I've finished the story, Rena."

"Honest? Gee, honey, I'm so proud of you! When are you gonna let me read it?"

"Next week some time." I examined the pattern in the wall paper. "You see, I'm leaving for Chicago tonight."

"What? You're leaving for——"

"Yeah. It's just for a couple of days. I've got to see that fellow I was telling you about. My agent. I've got to talk to him about my story."

"But gee, couldn't you write him, or phone, or something?"

I kissed her. "Don't you see, I'm no keener on this trip than you are, darling. But you know how important the story is to me. And I must talk to my agent in person, understand? After all, it's only two—three days."

"You're coming back? You wouldn't try to kid me?"

"What do you think? I'm moving right in. From now on it's you and me, just the way you want it. And when I get back, I won't do any writing the first week, either."

This seemed to be the signal for another clinch. In the middle of it she got an idea.

"Darling, you don't really have to go right away, do you? Tonight, I mean. Couldn't you take the train in the morning?"

"Well . . ."

"Why don't you lock the door?"

It sounded like a good idea.

I locked the door and Rena sat down on the sofa again and poured herself a drink. She gulped it and poured another.

"Get yourself a glass, honey. We're gonna celebrate."

I looked at her and grinned.

"So that's the way you feel, eh?"

"That's the way I feel."

I walked over to the sofa. "Then, before I get too involved, maybe I'd better give you what I brought you."

"Brought me?"

"Sure. Just a little going-away present."

I pulled it out of my suit-coat pocket and unfolded it.

"Oh, a scarf!"

I held it up to the light, holding an end in each hand.

"Like it?"

"Why, it's beautiful!"

"Here, let me put it on."

I draped it over her shoulders, pushing the pajama-straps low.

She kissed me. "You're so sweet, darling. Buying me a present. Yes. Take your coat off, honey. There. You know what your Rena is gonna do for buying her such a nice sweet present? You know what she's gonna do . . . ?"

"Darling, let me drape it for you."

"Drape?" She giggled.

I looped the scarf over her head and across her neck and pulled the ends free. I held one end in each hand and looked at her. She lay there staring up at me, her eyes shining. She was beginning to pant a little.

"Come on," she whispered. "Kiss me."

"Yes," I said. I bent down and kissed her. She put her arms around me, tight. I could feel her breathing into my mouth. I pulled on the ends of the scarf and jerked my head away.

II

THE hall was empty when I went downstairs. The street was deserted, too, and that suited me. I breathed in night air and strode quickly around the corner.

As I walked, I took off the gloves I'd worn upstairs and stuffed them into my suit-coat pocket. I could feel the bulge of the maroon scarf.

I jerked my hand away, fast, and sent it on another journey in search of a cigarette.

A few puffs helped a lot. When I saw a streetcar coming, I made the corner stop and climbed aboard.

My timing was just right. I got off in front of the depot ten minutes before train-time.

Nobody looked at me as I showed my ticket and lugged my bag down the platform, heading for the coaches. I got into a car. I found a vacant seat and eased into it.

Everything was quite simple, effortless. But I was sweating, and my legs were weak, and it wasn't until the train began to move that I could feel my heart slow down to normal.

There it was. Good-by, Minneapolis. Yes, and good-by Rena, too.

Good-by, Rena. . . .

I reached into my left-hand trousers pocket and pulled out the roll of bills I'd taken from her purse and from the jewel box behind her dressing-table. I held it down between my legs and counted quickly. Thirty-one twenties, sixteen tens, four fives, and three singles—eight hundred and three dollars in folding money. Not much, but it was enough.

"With all my worldly goods I thee endow."

Slipping the roll into my wallet, I sat back and stared out the window. All I could see was the red light of the Foshay Tower blinking off in the distance behind me.

As I turned away I caught my reflection in the glass. I had to look twice before I realized I was grinning. Well, why not? Why shouldn't I smile?

No need for me to worry now. There had been no noise, no struggle. I had put the gloves on when I searched for the cash.

I couldn't remember any other flaws. I'd played it smart, leaving the hotel yesterday instead of tonight. It would be hard, tracing Al Jackson—that was the name I'd signed. That was the only name Rena had known. Nobody else in town had ever asked who I was, or given a damn.

Besides, I doubted if there'd be much fuss. When they finally discovered her, everything would add up. Just another tramp found dead. Robbery. No signs of a struggle.

Or would there be? They could tell she was strangled. Some snooping newsie might be hard up for a yarn.

To hell with it. Water under the bridge. I paid for my ticket and I was taking my ride.

Meeting Rena in that tavern was just what the doctor ordered. A soft touch, with a husband doing time; money in the bank, and a fondness for playing spin the bottle. A pushover.

She had her own apartment and no steady friends. In less than a week she was begging me to move in with her.

I still don't know why I didn't. It would have been easy that way; but somehow I couldn't quite see myself actually living with a woman like Rena. Sharing a bed with one of those floppy French dolls; picking up hunks of red-stained Kleenex from the bathroom floor.

So I stalled. I took her rowing on Lake Harriet. I took her to taverns. I visited at her place, but not too often. A steady diet of her affection and I'd end up in an iron lung.

Rena couldn't understand why I preferred living in a dirty room downtown until I told her I was a writer.

That solved everything: why I didn't have a steady job, why I bummed around the country, why I was willing to take a few bucks from her but wouldn't settle down.

"I'm sort of your inspiration, ain't I?" she asked.

I almost hauled off and hit her.

Then it came to me in a flash. A flash of inspiration, I suppose.

"Maybe you've got something there. Rena, I think I'll write a story about you."

The minute she found out I was interested in the sad, sad story of her life, she went overboard. She began to bare her soul. Baring her body was all right—but the soul wasn't suitable.

I heard about the childhood in Duluth, everything. The drunken father and the mother with dropsy. The fumbling affair with some young football player. The Hollywood aspirations which ended in the arms of an Italian booking agent in St. Paul. The abortion. The year as a waitress, ending in marriage to Frankie Coleman, late of Fargo and now resident of State Pen. Then six months of drinking and just hanging around, climaxed by my entrance into the stirring drama.

Funny thing is, it did make a story—just a sketch about a day in the life of a little roundheels. Reproducing her conversation gave it the essential vulgarity of what passed for Rena's personality.

She was such a tramp, such a depressingly typical tramp, that changing names and places and a few minor details made it safe to use her story without sacrificing its authenticity.

But the ending stumped me. There was none. Here was Rena, without friends, connections, life-pattern; with no desire to learn or to become.

Her husband's money would be thrown away for drinks and her body would wither slowly between a hundred rumpled bedsheets. Rena would end up a drunken old floosie. Nobody gave a damn if she lived or died. The reader wouldn't care.

I didn't care.

I was sick of sponging off her, sick of keeping her amused. I was sick of the road, sick of the fast ramble, sick of writing with a stub pencil on stolen letterheads in dingy rooms.

Put them all together. Add ten years of living on the lam, riding empties, doing it the hard way. Throw in that ache—not loneliness, not ambition, but something else—the ache to tell somebody about it, put it down in writing and make it mean something. Yes, and multiply the factors, all the factors. I knew Rena had money stuffed away all around the apartment. I knew she was friendless. I knew it didn't matter what became of her.

Put them all together. And what do they spell?

Exactly what happened.

I sat there, riding the high iron through the night, and I tried to figure it out. But I knew I was lying to myself.

Sure, I wanted to be a writer. Sure, I needed Rena's money to get a flying start. But I didn't have to kill her, did I?

There are other ways to get money out of dames. I found out years ago that if you walk into a room, cold, and act as if you own the joint, nine times out of ten you get away with it and can issue orders. The approach works with men and it goes double with the women. Besides, there are all sorts of other angles. I didn't have to kill her for money.

Why kid anybody?

There's no sense trying to dress it up with fancy language and fake motivation: I killed Rena because she was just a story character to me. She wasn't real. She didn't exist at all. It wasn't as if she had friends, a family, a home.

Rena was somebody you drink with, talk with, sleep with, and all the while you're thinking of something else like finishing the yarn and getting it sold and getting up where you belong. You're no kid any more, you'll have to cut out this bumming around, taking it from everybody who wants to dish it out. You study her because for once you're really going through with it, you'll finish this one and sell it too, and all the while she keeps getting in your way and trying to make a two-bit pimp out of you. That's the whole secret, don't you see? You get her down on paper, where she can't hurt you any more, can't remind you of anyone—even herself. She's on paper, where she belongs. Where you can control her.

And then all that's left is this greedy, wet-kissing, sloppy bag, interfering with your life. The kind of a bag you're writing the story about. The kind that would end up dead in any story.

Then you realize that's the solution. That's the ending you've been looking for all along. So you sit down and work it all out on paper, just as if it was only a story. How you buy the tickets and pack and leave the hotel and go up there. You have the scarf and it seems appropriate, somehow, because you've always had the scarf. For ten years it's been the lucky charm.

Somehow, though, the luck has never worked. There have been so many chances: chances to get jobs, chances to get women, chances to get out of it all. Yes, and there have been so many other stories, too. Stories you didn't finish. Stories you couldn't finish. Why? Why hasn't the lucky charm worked?

You always wanted to do it. You wanted to show them. And then, at the last minute, something happened. You know what happened. You were afraid. You've been afraid of everything, for ten years. Running away, hiding away, kidding yourself about your lucky charm—the charm that doesn't work.

Maybe it's because you never *made* the charm work for you. Maybe you didn't know what it could do. What it could do if you wound it around somebody's neck and——

All right. This time you'll go through with it. And if you can, it proves that you are lucky. That there's nothing to be afraid of, no need to run away any more. Maybe if you have the guts you can carry on; finish your stories, quit pretending and come back into the world. Make contacts. Start going places.

Yes, the scarf is the right idea.

It works out on paper, and the minute you read it you know it's the only way. You can finish the yarn now. And you do it.

That's all. That's the pitch.

I was on the train, and in Chicago I'd mail my story in to an agent.

Good-by, Rena. . . .

I sat nodding in the coach, and jerked forward as the train rounded a curve.

Blinking, I reached for the overnight bag, opened it, and took out the manuscript.

I began to read it again. It sounded right to me. But when I got to the end, to the part where Rena died, I started to sweat.

The gesture was automatic. I reached into my pocket and pulled out something to wipe my forehead with.

It was the maroon scarf.

CHICAGO

III

When I hit Chicago, I lugged my bag over to the Castle Hotel. It was a ratty little dump, and the room I got wasn't much of an improvement over that fleabag in Minneapolis.

But I had to conserve my money. I needed time now: time to plan the next move, time to take stock of the situation.

I signed my own name on the register—Daniel Morley—and gave Milwaukee as the home address. I felt funny doing it, hadn't actually written my real signature in years. It seemed, somehow, like forgery. But from now on, I'd travel on the level, if my luck held. If——

Ten hours of sleep made a lot of difference. I got up around supper time, shaved, dressed, and went out to eat in a chop suey joint down the street. I picked up a *Daily News* and looked through it to see if there was any Minneapolis item about Rena Coleman. I couldn't find a thing.

I walked back over to the depot and got a copy of the Minneapolis *Star-Tribune*. There was no story in the early edition. So far, so good.

There was no reason for me to be nervous. There was no reason for me to stop in at that liquor store and pick up a pint. There was no reason for me to sit in my shabby little room and scrabble at the tinfoil, ram the bottle between my lips and gulp whiskey through teeth that just wouldn't stop chattering.

"Look," I said. "What are you afraid of?"

My voice bounced off the scaly plaster of the walls. A neon light below the window suddenly went on, and the blinker sent red and black flashes into my brain.

I closed my eyes and took another drink. When I opened them

again the alternation of red glare and deep darkness continued. Dot and dash. The broken thought persisted.

"What—are—you—afraid—of?"

Suddenly I stood up and set the bottle down on the table. This was it. I had to face it. Either I answered that question for myself once and for all, or I was through. Right back in the same old rut again. I'd drink up the eight hundred bucks and go back where I came from—running away. Running away from the question, and knowing at the same time I never could run quite far enough away.

All right. What was I afraid of?

Of being caught?

No, that was out. I'd covered my tracks pretty well. Nothing to worry about on that score.

Was I afraid of remembering what happened; *how* it happened?

I thought about that one for a while. It hadn't been so bad at all.

Rena had been surprised. Just surprised. She didn't have time to realize any stronger emotion. I was swift. The blood must have been cut off from her brain in a few seconds. Her face froze in surprise—not shock or fear.

Can this be happening to me? That's all she thought. I was sure of it. And it didn't bother me at all.

As a matter of fact, I was relieved. I'd brooded about it for so long—maybe everybody does—wondering what it must *feel* like. To be a murderer. To kill a woman.

You wonder what it does to you, are you afraid, do you know what you're doing, do you get any *pleasure* from it?

"You had to find out about it, didn't you?" I whispered. "You couldn't be satisfied until you found out. All right. All right, you morbidly curious, dirty-minded, smug, spineless, stupid little coward—you did find out!

"You thought it would be terrible, you never dreamed you could go through with the job, it was absolutely impossible. Then you did it. And you found out the truth.

"You found out that it didn't terrify you. That it was just like wringing the neck of a chicken.

"Sure, you were nervous. Who wouldn't be? Purely instinctive reaction. But beyond that, nothing. Nothing at all.

"And that's why you're afraid now. Not because you did it, not because you're a murderer.

"You're afraid because you're *not* afraid. Not afraid to kill, not afraid to do it all over again if you had to."

I nodded at my shadow on the wall. The shadow nodded back, then disappeared in a red glare.

I switched on the light and rummaged through my grip until I found what I was looking for.

It was a black loose-leaf notebook I'd picked up a few weeks ago when I was still taking notes on Rena. I hadn't used it, and that was good.

Because now I had another purpose in mind. I'd take a few notes on myself.

All right, maybe it sounds silly. But you have to tell somebody. You have to talk it out. Tell it to your wife, your best friend, your psychoanalyst, the neighbors, a priest, the bartender, a nice big fat Irish cop.

But I didn't have anyone to tell it to. About how I felt, what was going on inside. All I knew was that I had to reason it out, fast. Analyze. Find out what it was that made me feel this way.

I could have talked to myself. That's a good way. Lots and lots of lonely guys talk to themselves. You see them every day on South Dearborn Street in Chi—shuffling along in their ragged overcoats, patting the bulge of the rotgut bottle in the left pocket, talking to themselves. They've been doing it for years. And when they end up on a slab at the morgue their lips are still parted as though they were cut off in mid-sentence.

Not for me, thanks.

I'd write it out, work it out on paper. That was the safest way. The cathartic method, the books in the library called it. I'd picked up a lot of learning in public libraries in the last ten years.

But no more of that. From now on I was through with public libraries and public charity, too. I'd write it out, and then maybe I could think about the next move. About getting myself a job, actually hunting up an agent on the story, making a few contacts and starting to climb up where I belonged. It would all come true, this time I knew it. All I had to worry about was this fear inside me—this fear of myself.

What was the reason behind it? What made me tick?

I opened the notebook, took out a yellow Number 2 pencil, and started in.

The neon flickered. The naked bulb overhead gave off a hard dismal glare. My fingers ached. My back ached. My head ached. And finally my hand laid down the pencil, leaving a little puddle of sweat on the wood of the table.

Then I read what I'd written.

The Black Notebook

Maybe it all depends on how good a memory you have. Maybe it depends upon your capacity to cherish a hatred. Cherish it? You have to nourish it, make it grow into a beautiful red blossom. Then you inhale the scent, let it intoxicate you, overpower you. . . .

But that's not being honest with yourself. Let's get down to cases.

Take memories. . . .

Looking back, looking back and trying to figure what made you that way, several things stand out in your mind. There may have been more than several. Maybe there were a hundred. Maybe a thousand. Small events, little episodes, all pointing you in the same direction, so that you might think you had free will when you wobbled from side to side on the track, but there were no switches for you to throw, no turnings to choose.

Memories, like the time you were five years old and wet the bed, and your mother laughed at you. She made fun of you in front of the whole family while you ate Sunday dinner. You couldn't stand the snickering, and the way she described what you'd done. You ran from the table and vomited everything up. Only you couldn't vomit up one thing—the sudden hate, curling away in the pit of your stomach.

Your own mother! You wondered what she meant when she whined and whispered to you because you happened to pass the bathroom when your sister Geraldine was in the tub.

"What did you look at her for?" she asked. "Only nasty little boys look at little girls."

Then, memories of the day she caught you, behind the woodpile back of the house, playing Doctor—what the psychologists sweetly call "exploratory sex play"—with a little neighbor girl of your own age, which was nine. Your mother saw you, said you were filthy, ridiculed you, made your father switch you good and hard. She sold you thoroughly on the idea that sex was vile and shameful. You were a vile, filthy boy. You took it, dumbly, the way kids must, and that night at dinner she brought it up again, rubbing it in.

Later, hours later, you tossed on your bed, unable to sleep, because she'd tied your hands to the bedposts as punishment—to keep you, in her words, from polluting yourself—and because you didn't know exactly what she meant by vile and filthy. What was filthy? That meant dirty, didn't it? But the little girl had been clean and so had you.

Finally, overcome with thirst, you had slipped the bonds of ripped red flannel holding your wrists and had sneaked down the hall to the bathroom to get a drink of water. It was hot summer—you remember hearing the locusts singing and smelling the wild honeysuckle. Your parents' door was open and as you passed you saw and heard what they were doing, their nakedness and the panting. You remember that you fled back to your room, slipped back into the flannel bonds.

You remember the numb turmoil of your feelings; you didn't think; your conscious mind refused the whole thing. But then, she had called you filthy and she was filthy too!

You hated your mother from then on, although you didn't know then that it was hate. You had rejected her completely and she, sensing she'd lost a victory, sensing your coldness and loathing, took it out on you in constant and bitter nagging.

You knew you mustn't talk about it, mustn't think about it—even though she was always after you with questions. Prying. You weren't a pretty pair: the dumbly resentful son; the frustrated and antagonistic mother, unconsciously, unremittingly seeking revenge for something, not knowing what it was.

Many a time you whispered, "I'll kill you, you old bitch," and you meant it. Remember that? You meant it. If you had been big enough and strong enough, if somebody had even just handed you a gun and told you how to use it, you *would* have killed her.

You would have killed the school kids, too, when you were older—when you were in love with Lucille. The gang followed when you were walking home from school with her.

"Lookuh the big sissy, he's walkin' withis girl, walkin' withis girl. . . ."

You thought Lucille understood. You loved her with a terrible intensity. You were carrying around this load of love inside you, you had to place it somewhere, so you hung it on Lucille. You wrote that poem to her; that stupid, gushy poem; nothing but a childish scrawl on a piece of paper in which you wrapped your naked heart. She accepted it and read it and laughed at you, and even showed it to the other kids. You had always thought Lucille was a beautiful golden-haired little doll, all peaches and cream. But you knew what she was after she took your poem, and after Charley told you what she let him do that time after the party, you tore up your copy of the poem—tore up her filthy body and whispered, "I'll kill you, I'll kill you!"

Then you go through a period where your ideal is to be unliving and unfeeling.

And then there's Miss Frazer. Miss Frazer gets all your mother love. Miss Frazer props you up, has you coming out of yourself, very nearly makes you over. And then, one night, Miss Frazer fixes you, but good . . .

Ah, dear old golden childhood days!

Then all at once you're grown up. You don't feel any differently about things; you've merely learned to keep things hidden. You don't say, "I'll kill you!" any more. That is, not unless you're angry or drunk or think you're bigger than the other guy and can get away with it.

Sometimes you don't even say it to yourself any more. You don't admit the phrase exists.

But you get to wondering about other people. How do they feel about it? How do surgeons feel, and cops and judges and sheriffs and executioners?

They actually *do* kill people, sometimes. There's always a good reason: an accident, a necessity, a law. But do any of them feel the way you do?

Yes, are you the only one who has those thoughts?

Maybe you can get your murders from the movies. Or the radio programs. Or read the comic strips. The funny papers are full of killings.

Sounds a little sneaking, though, doesn't it—a little bit like masturbation, eh?

All right. Be a man. Let's face it. Go to football games and hope that "something happens." Attend prize fights and stand right up from your $40 seat to yell, "Murder the bum!" You mean what you're saying. Everybody means it. And it's OK. Nobody will arrest you. If you're lucky, and keep on going to enough fights, sooner or later you may actually see it happen.

See it happen. . . .

Don't worry. You'll get your opportunity, sooner or later. At motorcycle races, auto races, aviation shows. Go to the circus and wait for the acrobat to miss; wait for the wire-walker to fall at the carnival. Watch the death-defying lady in the lion's cage. What if the lion should close his rotten yellow fangs in her throat and . . . .

But it isn't the same as if *you* did it. It isn't the same as the real thing. And everybody secretly wants the real thing. They must.

Who does the other guy want to kill? His boss, his wife, his mother-in-law, the kids next door, the smart guy over him on the job, the butcher, the baker, the candlestick maker?

Why he wouldn't *think* of such a thing, would he? Not much he wouldn't!

Every time some motorist cuts in ahead of him while driving, every time somebody honks the horn when he crosses the street, every time he tries to sleep and those damned fools upstairs are throwing a party—he thinks of it.

He *must* feel the way you do about such things.

Sometimes you can remember way back to a face you've seen just casually—some fat, ugly old woman with a wart on her blotched and ruddy neck—and you wish to God you could plunge a knife right into the nastiness and watch the corruption spurt forth.

Sometimes you can remember an embarrassment, a humiliation, a slight or snub or ridicule ten years ago, and find that craving seethes up inside.

Don't you suppose the other guy has those moments, too?

Maybe that's what makes wars. But there's no use thinking about wars. It's such old stuff, and besides, a war is no good for *that* any more—lots of guys found it out the hard way. Only the hand-to-hand stuff, the machine guns, can give you the feeling you want.

All the rest is too impersonal, too mechanized; bombs and grenades, even flame throwers. It's just something you learn to do. Most of the time they say you can't even see it happen.

There's no thrill in an atomic bomb. The thrill must come when you see the blood, actually *feel* the life oozing away, wondering where it goes to, marveling at the power you gain.

But you must have the memories stored up; you must keep the hate inside.

Then almost anything can set it off. It doesn't necessarily have to be a person or an incident.

Sometimes a mood will do it. That awful, empty feeling you get on warm Sunday afternoons when the sky is muggy and gray. Heavy dinner, messy papers on the floor, somebody practicing the piano down the street, and nothing to do. Nowhere to go, no one to see. Emptiness. And tomorrow you go back to the grind.

Or try waiting in a small town railway waiting station at midnight. Make it in wintertime, when the wood-stove is smoking, when the musty, dead smell wells up all around you, and the hard, whittled-up bench is strewn with dirty orange peels. Stare into the gobby, spit-filled cuspidor, stare at the chewed-up dung of a cigar butt. And wait for the train, the train that's late, the train that's never coming, the train that will take you back to the place you don't want to go to.

Lie awake in a hospital bed at four in the morning. Watch the gray stealing along the corridors. Listen to the moans. Hear the dryness of a death-rattle, the cricket chirping merrily in the throat of a corpse. Think about yourself, about your own chances of recovery, think about getting well, getting out of there and going back to the life you've tried to escape from.

But why be morbid? Why deliberately cut yourself off from the world and make things miserable? It isn't a bit necessary.

Go to a night club, or a ballroom. Go to the Lonely Hearts Hall. Get out and have a little fun.

Watch the beefy, red-necked, gum-chomping, bristle-headed, horny young sailors fumbling the breasts of sallow-faced, skinny, fish-eyed, clown-painted little girls. See the sleek-haired pimps talking second-generation English to fat, hennaed, giggling women. Visit the sly and slinking Negro queer in the men's john. Look at the twisted mouth of the dying snowbird who plays tenor sax in the combo. Gaze into the boiled red sheep's eyes of the hairless bouncer.

Look at that shriveled-up old tramp over there, she must be feeble-minded, trying to make that shy young kid with the glasses. See that old guy, watch his hands tremble, what's he doing up here? Oh, he's turning around, his face is burned. There's a real treat for you, that pretty girl over there—the young one. She doesn't belong here. But she's with that pock-marked guy, socking it in. Everybody's out for a good time here, having lots of laughs. Getting drunk and sneaking feels and making dates; forgetting their troubles. It's a party, it's dancing, music, gaiety; they've got the world by the oysters.

What's the matter, you think you're better than these people, or something? Why, most of them make more money than you do, lots of them are nicer looking, and one thing is certain—they're having a damned sight better time than you are.

That's it, isn't it? You wonder why it is they can all enjoy themselves and you aren't having any fun.

Or are you thinking: yes, these are people, a pretty ordinary crowd of people at that. They pay taxes, they vote, they make the laws, they choose the popular songs and the books and the pictures, they tell us all how to live and how to work and what to think and worship. Yes, and if they were on your jury, your life would be in their hands.

Is that the way you figure it? Do you wish, as you watch them dancing, that you could walk right up to the bandstand and take out a sub-machine gun and let 'em have it, just mow 'em down; the whole cruel, greedy, moronic, dirty lot of them?

Maybe I'm wrong.

Maybe most people *don't* have those thoughts, those feelings, those desires.

Maybe it's just people like me.

Maybe they'd be afraid of me if they knew what went on inside. I must never let them find out. Write it all down, but don't tell anybody.

But I'd like to tell them. I'd like to let them know how I feel. How *it* feels. The whole works. I'd like to give them all a little personal demonstration. With my scarf.

And their necks. . . .

IV

I SLEPT that night as if I'd been drunk for a week, but in the morning I felt fine. I felt even finer after another trip to the depot and another checkup on the Minneapolis paper. There wasn't a line about Rena, and maybe there never would be.

So I had breakfast and walked over to the Star Cab Company and filled out an application for driving.

Maybe, at first thought, it doesn't make sense—starting out to climb by becoming a hackie. But one thing I learned on the road; if you want to make contacts you have to get people to notice you.

One way of doing it is by putting on a phony front. But that takes money, and at least a few friends. I knew where I wanted to go, all right—I had to get in with a crowd of writers, editors, publishers. But I couldn't come in through the front door, cold. Not yet, anyhow. Even a magazine office has employment forms to fill out, and I wasn't equipped to give the right answers to their questions. For a cab company I had answers.

Hacking is good for contacts. I'd done it before in St. Louis, and it paid off. I can't exactly figure out why, but somehow people always notice cab drivers. Nobody looks at a waiter, or a bellboy, or a mooching salesman. But cabbies get the breaks. They get the talkative drunks, they run into the unusual situations. People ask them questions: how did you get into this racket, what's new in town, buddy, where can you fix me up with a broad?

Besides, if I was going to write, I'd need that kind of a job. Something that gave me regular hours without a lot of rules and restrictions; a spot where I could think. Driving nights would leave me with my afternoons free to write, when I felt fresh.

In two days, I was on. There isn't much to tell about the job itself. I played the Loop for the lushes, and did all right. Inside of a month I was out of the Castle Hotel and in an apartment over on North Clark. No palace, but a step in the right direction.

Days, I'd sleep until ten or eleven, go out and have breakfast, then come back to my place for a session of work. I rented a typewriter, but I didn't write.

I read.

There was so much to read. As a kid I'd been a bookworm. Then, when I—went away from school—reading was out. I picked up the habit again by going into public libraries to keep warm. When I resumed interest in writing I began to read a bit more deliberately—selectively.

But it wasn't enough. It wasn't anywhere near enough. I found that out. I had to read more. Current stuff, classics, non-fiction, everything. I took out a library card and carried books home day after day, for weeks. Inside of a month or so I'd knocked off nearly sixty books.

I was making progress.

And I was bored as hell.

I still hadn't sent out my story. Partly because I was a little unsure of it, but mostly because I didn't know where to send it. The sharpies who advertised for suckers in the magazines wouldn't do me any good. No sense in sending the yarn out cold, either, to a random market. What I needed was a good agent.

Also a few good drunks and a few good women. . . .

But that was out.

At least, I figured it that way until I met Hazel Hurley.

The people that ride in taxicabs! The things they do in them!

In three months I saw more of life in the raw than I'd managed to pick up in ten years of knocking around. And I kept looking. Looking for material, yes, but also looking for that contact—for that big chance to open up, give somebody the business, make an impression. I studied the loads I got, sized up each situation. I knew that sooner or later something was bound to pop. The law of averages was on my side. Only a question of time, so keep your eyes open buddy, make with the smile. . . .

The rear-view mirror is a great invention.

Hazel Hurley showed up in it one night around eleven, fresh out of the Pump Room.

She wore a black, low-cut dress and elaborate pendant earrings. Her red hair stood out like a flame, and half a dozen male moths fluttered around on the sidewalk. A particularly fat and oily insect lurched over and entered the cab with her.

"Hotel Cheltenham."

They were quarreling. I didn't care about that, at first. But I kept watching Hazel Hurley.

She was a beautiful hunk of woman. You never realize how they kick that word "beautiful" around until you see someone like her. The bones of her face. Even her skull would be beautiful.

Somewhere along the line she must have caught me staring at her in the mirror. She winked.

I winked back.

Then we were both laughing like hell. It didn't matter, because the moth had passed out by this time, after a particularly bad session over the edge of the window.

She was just tipsy enough to enjoy sitting there with her feet curled up under her on the seat, giggling like a kitten over cream.

You've heard of love at first sight?

Well, love had nothing to do with it.

Of course I had to carry the boy friend inside. She wanted no part of that deal any more; the quarrel had told me that.

A veddy veddy suave bell captain took charge of the lush and paid me off. He even added a tip. I went back to the cab and she was still sitting there.

Her smile told me it was tailor-made. This might be the break, if I worked it right.

I climbed into the cab, shut the door, and pulled away.

"Thanks for taking care of him," she said.

I nodded, without turning around, and kept going.

She tapped me on the shoulder. I cocked my head.

"You want to know where we're going, is that it?

"Well, frankly, lady, if it's all right with you, I'd like to stop in for something to eat. I'm starved."

That, although she didn't know it, was the works. If she said no, I was sunk. If she said yes. . . .

She said yes.

I'd figured it right. Seven or eight Martinis, the world is rosy, you've just gotten rid of a fat bore, and the night is still young.

Besides, it's so gay and bohemian to do something like this once in a while, and you'll be careful. . . .

I had her number.

She got mine by looking at the identification card and the cheap dime-store photo they made you stick on it.

"Daniel Morley, isn't it?"

"Dan."

"All right, Dan, let's go."

We went. Five minutes later we were playing footie at a table in Tony's.

Hazel Hurley was a free-lance model, and she had been doing a lot of work for the man who had passed out in the cab. She didn't say what kind of work. I didn't ask.

Then she mentioned the man's name—Berton Bascomb, of Bascomb, Collins and Associates, Advertising.

That did it. My hunch was paying off. Now was the time to start working.

A girl who has just walked out on a Bascomb doesn't go for taxi-drivers, even on the rebound. But she might go for a writer, even if he had a hard-luck label pinned on his trousers. I could find out, anyway.

I'd carried the book around in my jacket-pocket for over a month, just waiting. Now I pulled it out and pretended to read until the food arrived.

"What's that?"

I showed it to her, waited for the giggle, got it.

"I'm sorry. But I didn't know taxi-drivers read Proust."

"Who said I'm a taxi-driver?"

"But——"

"I'm a writer," I told her. "Ever hear of picking up local color?"

Right now the local color I wanted to pick up was red, but she didn't have to know everything. She was going to find out the hard way.

The drink that arrived with our food helped to start her off. From that time on I didn't do much talking. I listened.

So I was a writer. How thrilling, because Hazel, too, wanted to write. She had so many exciting experiences as a model and she just knew there was a good novel in them. All those temperamental photographers and screwball—just screwball—art directors and wolves that made passes at hardworking career girls—why it was just thrilling! And wherever she went, Hazel jotted down little mental notes of human interest, because she felt human interest was so important in a good book, and didn't I agree?

I opened my mouth, but the timing was off. She told me what an interesting life I must lead, because she felt that all writers must lead such interesting lives. Observing people constantly made authors feel something like God, didn't I think so?

I managed to tell her that I didn't feel like God, I felt like another drink.

She giggled as I ordered. I didn't go for the giggle. But I did like what I could see of her—which, in that dress, was plenty. And in the back of my mind, the hunch was working.

Some obliging soul had just fed the juke-box. I made a gallant gesture.

"Care to dance?"

We danced.

You can learn a lot about a woman by dancing with her, if you know what to look for. You can gauge the pressure of her arm against your back, notice whether her fingers dig into your shoulder or lie flat and outstretched. You can watch the way she holds her head; note if she looks up at you, or gazes off over your arm, or snuggles her head down against your chest.

Her footwork doesn't matter much; it's the other things that count. And you don't have to be Freud to analyze what she does with her hips.

I learned a lot about Hazel when I danced with her. And I learned a few things about myself, too.

I found out I wanted to hold her because I needed something to hang on to—something more solid than memories of Rena. When I felt her waist under my fingers I forgot Rena completely, and it made me realize how much I had *wanted* to forget her.

Yes, Hazel Hurley was what I needed. The problem was how to get her—fast.

Flattery wouldn't work. Hazel ate up flattery, of course, but you don't fall in love with what you feed on.

In just a few dances I managed to decide she was selfish as hell, flighty as hell, but above all, vain. Her idea of a great work of art was a mirror.

Whatever she did, she dramatized herself. And that was my cue. I could hear her telling the story to her friends:

"And after Berton passed out, this cab-driver came back and pulled away from the curb without a *word*. . . . imagine! . . . of course he'd been *looking* at me *all* evening . . . *you* know . . . and then he asked me would I mind . . . it was a perfectly *vile* little dive . . . he pulled this book out, and I thought I'd *die* . . . yes, I said *Proust!* . . . a writer, darling, and it turns out he was just looking for local color. . . ."

Yes, I knew the way she'd tell the story. But it was up to me to supply a proper ending. The ending I wanted.

Keeping her on the dance floor, I began feeding her a version of my life. My struggles against fate, adversity, the cruel chains of environment.

"Then you really have to drive a cab for a living?"

"Oh, I write a little on the side. But mostly I do it sitting up."

That was the wrong note. I switched back to my routine. How I'd been trying to get a decent job so I could break into full-time writing.

"But why don't you *get* a decent job, Dan? You have the ability, the education——"

"Try telling that to some fat-faced executive," I said, with a brave little smile on my face. "You see, whatever I know, I've picked up for myself, the hard way. I've never gone to college, never held a responsible position. I can write, yes. I can probably do a better job than most university-trained men. As you so cleverly pointed out, I know people. But I don't seem to know the *right* people."

"You're a very strange man, Dan. I've never met anyone quite like you."

"Just a hack driver who wants to become a hack writer."

"Where do you live?"

"Is this a proposition?"

"Don't be absurd. I've got an idea, Dan, and maybe I can work it out. I'd like to be able to get in touch with you by phone in a few days."

"Good girl." I smiled down at her, tenderly. "And I suggest you tell Mr. Bascomb that I'm very good at writing radio continuity."

V

WHEN Hazel called me, three days later, I was prepared. I handed in my resignation to the Star people, removed my leather jacket, and returned the Proust to the library.

Then I put on my brown suit and went down to Bascomb, Collins and Associates.

I didn't see Bascomb, I didn't see Collins, and I didn't see any associates. Apparently everything had been set up for me. Whatever Hazel Hurley had on Berton Bascomb, she knew how to use it.

Ten minutes after I stepped into the chromium bleached mahogany glassbricked fluorescent-lighted empire, I was a radio continuity writer at seventy-five per, to start. I occupied a tiny cubicle four doors down the hall from my immediate chief, Lou King. And that's the whole deal, ready for the nutshell.

Lou King was a right guy and asked no embarrassing questions. First thing, they put me to work doing a bunch of 100-word spot announcements for a beer client. Small fry, just to try me out.

I spent a day or so nosing around the place, reading stacks of old continuity, and trying to get a line on what made the wheels turn. Then I gagged up a couple of trick openings and copied virtually the same patter used by the last man on the assignment.

Nobody said anything, but I heard on the grapevine that the stuff was approved for use and went on the air without changes.

I was in. The receptionist at the outer desk began to give me a friendly sniff when I passed, and I began to learn how to get around the layout without using a compass.

They gave me another batch of radio spots for a kitchen soap, and just on the off-chance I rapped out a little idea for a singing-commercial. You know the stuff—two sopranos warbling:

We're the happy Kleeno bubbles
Washing away all your troubles
Put some Kleeno in your tub
No more worry, rub or scrub
Get
KL-EEEEEEEEEEEEE-N-OOOOOO!

What the hell, they say it's the oldest profession. And I didn't have to listen to it, did I?

After the conference with the soap people and the transcription agency they brought in to wax the jingle, I got a real enclosed office of my own and a batch of new jingle assignments. King was very pleased, and learned to remember my name.

I didn't mix much with the copy gang. Compared to most of them, I was working for peanuts, so I steered clear of the five o'clock sessions in the cocktail bar downstairs. Dishing out wise shop-talk with account executives is risky business. That I'd have to practice.

My best bet was to cultivate Lou King. I managed to run into him several times at lunch, and got the habit established. One day I figured the time was ripe to steer the conversation around to writing.

That scored with him. He made five hundred a week "analyzing copy" but he couldn't write a catch phrase on a lavatory wall.

He'd never asked me how I managed to get my job without jumping through the hoops of an application blank and the usual aptitude tests. Apparently he had his suspicions. But now, the knowledge that I was a writer threw him off the beam again. He began to believe that I'd been "scouted" for this job and was probably a secret protégé of Bascomb's. Consequently he warmed up considerably and we talked for over an hour.

Funny thing—I don't seem to make many friends. But Lou King was the kind of a guy I could be friendly with. Even though I was dishing out a line, I could still react to his naïve interest. He wanted to know what I'd been writing lately.

I brought down my story about Rena and showed it to him the next day at lunch. He got excited.

"Where are you peddling it?" he asked. "It's too highbrow for the regular slicks. What about the quality books—say the *Atlantic,* or *Harpers*?"

"Well, I don't know. I was thinking of locating myself a good agent, to begin with."

"Phil Teffner!" he yelled.

"Who?"

"Phil Teffner. You're a writer and you don't know Teffner? He's one of the top ten in the racket. Movie rights, the book clubs, reprints, special editions for Zanzibar, the works!"

"What would he want with little old me?"

Lou King smiled benevolently. "He's a good friend of mine, or was, once. I used to hang around his office in New York, years ago. And I think——"

I waited, patiently.

"Tell you what I'll do, Dan. Give me the yarn and I'll send it in with a note. He only handles big names, but I can introduce you. If he smells a sale, he'll handle it. Where you been selling your stuff?"

I played it straight and admitted I hadn't sold anything yet. "But I'm working on this sort of thing right along. Fact is, I took this job so I'd have time to knock out some fiction on the side."

"Good. Teffner's a smart operator. He wants a stable full of steady producers, not one-shots. I'll give him a build up about how you sit up nights pounding out literature and he'll bite."

What I was doing nights was not exactly pounding out literature. Hazel wasn't that kind of a girl.

Naturally, I'd been seeing her right along. The minute I got the job I called her and we had dinner.

Seeing me in that brown double-breasted suit made her sit up and take notice. By the time the evening was over, I made it pretty clear to her that she hadn't fallen for a taxi-driving bum because she happened to run into him when she had a snootful.

I thanked her for the lead, but didn't tell her anything about the job. That was still a little too intimate a subject for this stage of the game.

A few nights later I managed to bring it up, and she set me straight.

"It was a favor, Dan," she told me. "That big ape owes me a

few favors. Besides, he has a wife—oh, forget it! There's only one thing I want to make clear—I'm all through with him, and he knows it. I'm back with my girl friend at the apartment."

She was telling me something else there, and she knew I knew it.

"I hope your girl friend works nights," I said.

"Funny thing, she does." Giggle.

"Funny thing," I said.

"Dan."

"Hmmm?"

"Why so quiet?"

"Thinking."

"What about?"

"Guess."

"Me?"

"You're really on the beam tonight."

"Tell me."

"I was thinking that you are the kind of a girl who would wear an ankle bracelet. For the right man."

She thought it was a compliment.

We had plenty of brilliant conversations like that one, liberally punctuated with giggles. Truth to tell, Hazel Hurley was no Madame Récamier. But she was luscious, and I was young, and the moon was mellow—you can see what I mean.

Also, I was beginning to figure out how she could help me. That job was only the beginning. I needed other things.

Came the night we went out on the town.

I didn't tell her anything, just made the date and told her to drape herself in her best.

She did, and we went into action.

Hazel had her faults, but she was definitely a show piece. Everywhere we went, I could feel the eyes turning; a sudden blink as that flaming halo of hair came into view, and then the slow, intent stare burning into her body. A hundred men mentally murdered me.

I knew she was eating it up, and I fed on it too. We were both in a good mood, and the drinks helped.

We were dancing when I broke it to her.

"Why are we celebrating, Dan?"

"Because we just sold a story today." I told her where, and for how much.

"You did!" She squeezed me and waited to be kissed, but not for long.

"*We* did," I corrected her. "If it hadn't been for meeting you, I'd never have written the darn thing." She didn't have to know I brought the yarn to town with me.

She giggled.

"What's that for?"

"Because I'm happy."

"Phil Teffner—that's my agent—says they want more, too."

"That's wonderful, Dan."

I shrugged. "Not so wonderful. Because it means I'll have to settle down and go to work, now. No more nights like this one for a while. I've got to stay home and turn out some writing."

"But think of the opportunity you have."

"I'm thinking of the opportunities I'll miss—with you."

"Don't talk that way, Dan. You give me ideas."

"I like your ideas, if they're practical."

"I don't know."

A couple of drinks later we decided to find out.

One thing I must say for Hazel Hurley—she had a lovely apartment.

Several hours later I was smoking a cigarette in bed and wondering why it is that the girls with the most beautiful bodies invariably become models and conceal those bodies beneath clothes. Then another thought hit me. It must have been percolating in there a long time, because there was a naturalness, an inevitability about it.

But it hit me suddenly, and hit me hard.

I sat up in bed and poked Hazel in the ribs.

"What is it, darling?"

"Know something?" I said. "I think I'm going to write a book."

"A book?"

"Yes, Hazel. A book—about you."

VI

DON'T ask me to explain it. Three months before I'd been a drunken bum. Now I was a novelist.

I can't analyze it. You can buy a three-dollar book on writing that will interpret the process for you in sesquipedalian terms. Me, I still have to look up words like "sesquipedalian."

But it happened. I was writing, every night. Writing with ease and assurance. I turned out an average of ten pages an evening, counting revision. In six weeks I was more than halfway through *Queen of Hearts.*

Actually, I suppose there's no trick in writing a salable novel about a woman. Take one Cinderella, add a dash of cynicism, sprinkle with sex episodes, mix ten drops of soap opera, and there you are. The plot is strictly Horatio Alger, but instead of Dan the Bootblack you substitute Doris, the Beautiful Car Hop. The old ugly duckling, rags-to-riches formula.

It was all Hazel, every page of it. The self-conscious way she patted her hair at the nape of her neck, when she knew somebody was looking. Her intent little frown as she applied make-up to her lips. The surreptitious glance down at her nylons when she rose from a chair. The way the dusting powder clung to the inner seams of her dresses around the armpits. The key and tempo of her giggle.

I merely had to close my eyes and remember it all. There was a little of Rena in it, too; but most women are essentially alike. Not a very profound statement, and yet they pay you good money to restate it in terms of a novel.

You don't need total recall to visualize the stockings hanging to dry on the edge of the washbowl; the mashed cigarette butt, its end bleeding into the ash tray; the aphrodisiac odor of a woman's purse.

I found I could write literate English; even the dialogue was grammatically correct. Phony as hell, too.

I used to worry about that. Why it was that book-talk differed so radically from actual conversation or even actual verbal thought, where the vernacular holds sway and most sentences are left unfinished. Those long, brilliant disquisitions delivered by characters always puzzled me. I'd never heard any two-page impromptu monologues from any of my friends.

Then I decided, (a) I didn't have the right kind of friends, and (b) to hell with it—if that's the way they want it written, that's the way I'll write it.

So *Queen of Hearts* came alive under my fingers, every word a jewel, and I knew it was corny and felt pretty certain it would please Teffner and some publisher and plenty of women just as shallow and idiotic as Hazel Hurley.

Hazel was proving to be more than shallow and idiotic—she was also persistent, and a damned nuisance.

She knew I was writing a book "about her" of course. And telling her *that* was my biggest mistake.

She got into the habit of coming up to the apartment almost every night. I didn't worry about appearances; the place I lived, you could bring a horse in and nobody would ask any questions.

But Hazel wasn't a horse. She was a woman, a highly articulate woman. And she was definitely getting in the way of my book.

She was turning out to be much more of a problem than Rena. Rena wanted only one—or, at the most, two—things, and the second was liquor.

Hazel wanted attention, flattery, and reassurance. She had ideas about writing, too, and now that she was my inspiration she intended to keep on inspiring me.

You'd think I was doing the book on marijuana, and that she kept a package of reefers under the sheets to give me a jolt.

Even though she had dropped Bascomb, she still got plenty of modeling calls, but there were days when she had no appointments. She took to coming in and straightening up the place; some evenings she'd go out and buy groceries and have supper ready when I got home from the office. I think I could have swung a deal to get my socks darned if I'd been in there pitching.

"Darling, I don't know what you've got." Then she giggled. "I've never done these things for a man before."

She was telling the truth. Up to now, she'd done only one thing for the men she knew—and it would have suited me if she'd confined her activities to that with me.

But there's nothing worse than a glamour girl gone domestic. The fussing and fluttering got on my nerves. She kept after me about my diet, about smoking, about getting enough rest. You'd think she was grooming me for a Dog Show.

Evenings, when I typed, she'd curl up in a chair and try to read. She kept waiting for me to show her the stuff I'd I turned out. I was careful not to let her see anything. A few helpful comments from Hazel would fix everything.

Along about mid-February I began to get stuck. I had my outline for the remaining chapters all set, but the stuff turned sour on me. I got down to four or five pages a night. Sometimes I tore them up. Sometimes I couldn't seem to do anything.

My resentment of Hazel turned against my heroine. I found myself hating her. I felt that perhaps she didn't deserve the happy ending I'd planned. Her habits and mannerisms, her outlook on life annoyed me.

Sometimes the things I made her say and do gagged me. I couldn't put them down. It was hard for me to remember that she was a beautiful woman, desirable, charming.

Finally I stopped, cold. I had about fifty thousand words of manuscript, so I bundled it up and sent it off to Teffner with a letter, asking for suggestions and comment.

The decks were cleared for action now. That night, when Hazel showed up, I got ready for a good fight.

Did you ever try to punch a raw oyster? That's the way it was, fighting with Hazel Hurley. She took everything I had, and she didn't giggle. She cried.

Of course I was right. She had no business hanging around and interfering with my work. She didn't blame me for hating her. I wasn't like other men, and I could see through her looks and realize she was just a silly, stupid girl.

It was the last thing in the world she'd ever intended to do, spoiling my career, and she'd make it up to me if only I'd forgive her for her thoughtlessness and blundering. Yes, she would clear out and let me finish the novel in peace, and I mustn't worry because no matter what happened she'd wait for me. She never intended to interfere with me, whatever I did—I'd see that she would never make any trouble, even after we were married.

She left, tearfully penitent, and that word, "married," kept echoing and re-echoing through the room. It took me two days and a gallon of liquor to drown it out.

The thing that sobered me up was Teffner's answer to my letter. He sent a telegram:

GREAT STUFF JUST KEEP IT UP HAVE NIBBLE FROM FIRST LINE PUBLISHER ON BASIS OF SUBMITTED MANUSCRIPT AND OUTLINE CAN YOU FINISH ON OR BEFORE APRIL FIRST REGARDS TEFFNER

No, it wasn't bad for a guy fresh out of the gutter; a publisher nibbling at an unfinished book, a soft job, and a genuine model for a girl friend.

Only I didn't want the girl friend any more. And I was beginning to find out that I didn't want the job, either.

It was easy money, and they liked me, and I knew I was set to go places. But it interfered with my writing, just as Hazel did. And somehow, that telegram was the clincher—I knew I was going to stick to writing, come what might.

What was to stop me from finishing the book, chucking the job, and going to New York?

Hazel.

But what if she didn't know I'd quit my job? But how could I quit and not have her find out about it within three hours? She was as close to the agency racket in town as I was.

There wasn't any way. Unless, of course, I walked out right now, changed my address so she couldn't find me, and then finished the book in peace.

Why not? What with the writing at night and the home-cooked meals, I'd managed to put away several hundred—in addition to most of my original stake from Rena. I could keep going for months on that kind of money, if I had to.

And it was now or never, if I expected to get Hazel out of my life. Why is it that women have to mother you, make you over, suffer for you? Why can't they let you alone? I might as well admit it. I was afraid of Hazel Hurley. I can understand why they speak of a person "growing" on you, because Hazel was growing on me; creeping, twining, clinging, putting out feelers, enfolding and choking and stifling me.

I had a nightmare about a Medusa with red serpent locks, locks that coiled about me and strangled as a wet mouth pressed mine. And all the while Medusa was giggling.

The day before I quit I got a room out near Garfield Park and moved the typewriter and suitcase over.

Then I managed a lunch date with King. I didn't waste any time in small talk, but got right down to business. "Lou, I wanted you to be the first to know."

"Expecting a baby?"

"Sort of. I've written a book."

"Novel? Dammit, that's great!"

"Matter of fact, your boy Teffner has it sold already."

"Say, this calls for a little drink, doesn't it? Your stock ought to go way up at the office. Having an honest-to-God writer on the staff will make Bascomb happy."

"He isn't going to be happy, Lou. And that's why I wanted to talk to you, first."

"What gives?"

"I'm quitting, Lou."

"You crazy or something?"

"I'll settle for something. Look, pal—let's not kid each other. I'm a writer, not a verbal sound-effects man. I've always wanted to do a book, and then another book, and then another. Well, I'm on my way."

Lou King shrugged.

"Look, Dan. It's none of my business, I suppose, but listen to me for a minute. You're young. You've got a helluva good start in this business. Marquardt and I have plans for you—next season an assignment on all our west-coast stuff; not just jingles and spots but half-hour shots. You can knock down good dough handling scripts. You'll still have plenty of time for writing. What the hell, you did this novel in your spare time, didn't you?"

"But——"

"That's not all, brother. Did you ever stop to think of this angle? Thousands of guys are beating their brains out every year writing books. Every broken-down hack that ever had a job on a newspaper or in advertising sooner or later gets the idea that he's going to write the Great American Novel. And hundreds of the damn fools actually do write their books and get them published, every year.

"How many of those hundreds of novels have you read this year? How many do you think anybody has read?

"Get the pitch? Teffner can tell you much better than I can—there's no money in writing unless you get the breaks. Unless you build up a name, hit the book clubs or the movies with a sale.

"You can starve to death in that racket, son. And here's another encouraging thought: you've written one book, but how do you know you can write another? The woods are full of one-book authors. Maybe you're the exception. Maybe you're different, I don't know. But I think you're way off the beam there."

"Teffner doesn't," I lied. "It was his idea. He wants me close at hand. He can sew up the usual three-book contract and guarantee me promotion on it. Then he has some stuff lined up on assignment. Sure-fire. But I'll have to be in New York to work with him."

"Then why don't you play it this way? Go to Bascomb and tell him all about it. Like I say, the idea of having a book-author in the agency is something he'll go for in a very large way. He'll spot the publicity value of the deal at once.

"Ask him for a leave of absence—with pay, because he'll buy that deal—and go to New York for a couple of months. Get yourself lined up. Then come back here and work."

I shook my head and looked sad.

"It wouldn't be fair," I said. "Not to Bascomb, and not to Teffner, and not to myself."

"I'm not talking fairness. I'm talking common sense. I just can't figure out why you'd throw everything up this way. You're young, you've got a good deal at the office, you're running around with the hottest little——"

This I was waiting for.

"Not any more," I sighed. "Lou, just between us, I guess that's the real reason I want to get away."

"You mean you and Hazel are through?"

"I'm afraid so. It's the old gag—you can't work on a woman and a novel at the same time."

"But can't you patch it up or something?"

I shook my head. "It would always be that way," I told him. "I'd want to continue with my work and she'd object. We'd be right back in the same routine.

"There's only one answer for me. Get away. Forget her. I don't even want to see her again; don't want her to know I've left. That's why I want to quit cold—and fast. And that's why I need your help. You can do it for me, if you're willing, I know that. How soon can I get out of the office, Lou? Without anybody asking questions?"

"Why, right away. I can fix it up. But I still wish you'd change your mind. We could do a lot together, Dan. You and I see eye to eye on things."

I held out my hand.

"See what you can do for me, pal," I said. "I'm counting on you."

At nine the next morning I was sitting in my room, looking out at Garfield Park and pounding away on the novel.

I've never yet read a convincing explanation of the magic that goes on inside a man's mind when he's writing. Near as I can figure out, it's like a run of luck in poker; for no reason at all, the cards begin coming your way, you play your hand automatically, confident that you'll fill your straight or get that third ace.

That's as close as I can come to it, and that's how it worked out for me.

When you're really playing poker and the stakes are high, there's no worry about what's going on around you—the kibitzers, the interruptions, the noises. You don't seem to need to eat or sleep.

What I'm trying to say is, I finished the rest of that novel inside of three weeks and shipped it off to Teffner. Apparently he hadn't been handing me any line about how hot his publishers were, because I got back an O.K. within two weeks.

I didn't know it at the time, but I guess that's some kind of a world's record for a novice. It looked, though, as if my luck was holding.

Teffner's lengthy letter mentioned revisions and corrections. I promptly wired him that I'd be leaving for New York on March 15, and would be ready to make changes on the spot.

Everything was set. I hadn't stirred from my room except when I took a turn around the block to stretch my legs, or pick up a meal and a package of cigarettes. Nobody knew where I was living, and there hadn't been any trouble with Hazel.

If I left town now, there never would be trouble. For once I had the satisfaction of actually carrying a job through to its ultimate conclusion, and doing it clean.

I began to think about packing. I still had about eight hundred bucks, counting my final pay from the office—and there was an advance on the novel waiting for me in New York. I could buy clothes when I got there, and leave my dirty linen behind. Symbolic gesture.

Ten years of dirty linen to leave behind me. Ten years of flops, soiled and ragged memories. It was a complete break with the past—a break from Rena, from the Star Cab Company, Bascomb, Collins and Associates, Lou King, Hazel, everything.

I gathered my effects on the bed and considered them. The black notebook caught my eye. I hadn't made an entry in it since that first bad night in the crummy hotel. Perhaps I would never make another.

From now on I was Daniel Morley, novelist, by God! I could do it—I had done it—without liquor, or women, or a phony line. From now on, I'd always be able to do it. If my luck held.

My luck was holding, up until the afternoon of the twelfth, when Hazel Hurley knocked on my door.

VII

"So you thought you'd run out on me."

"Now wait a minute, Hazel——"

"Don't wait-a-minute me! I know all about it. King told me this morning at the agency how you'd quit your job and gone to New York. I knew it was a lie the minute I heard it, because what *he* didn't know is that your book isn't finished yet."

"But——"

She must have been rehearsing the monologue for hours, because I couldn't stop her. And from the look on her face it wasn't a very good idea to try.

"I suppose you're wondering how I found out where you'd sneaked off to? Well, I'm going to tell you—so that next time you can be a little more careful covering your tracks. If there is a next time.

"You thought you were pretty clever, not leaving any forwarding address, didn't you? But you did tell the people at the typewriter agency where you'd moved to, when you rented the machine for another month. I just happened to remember about the typewriter and called them up."

"Clever girl."

"You're damned right I'm clever, Dan. A little bit too clever to fall for any more of your phony pitches. *You* were going to look me up when your book was finished. You were going to make good on the job and get married!

"What a cheap, two-timing heel you turned out to be! Quitting your job and hiding out here just to get rid of me—you couldn't tell me you were through, like a man. Always playing the big shot! Even when you ran out on me you had to cover up with that dirty lie about selling your book!"

Seeing her angry like this, striding up and down with her bracelets banging and her breasts strutting out, I could almost go for her all over again. But there was something else I had to do.

"All right, wise guy—got anything to say for yourself? Or should I give you a little more time to cook up a new story? You're good on stories."

I sighed.

"Yes, Hazel, you're right. I'm good on stories. Here. Look at this."

I fished Teffner's telegram out of my coat and handed it to her.

"There, you can see for yourself. I've sold the book!"

That stopped her, cold.

"I finished the damned thing and sold it. I wasn't lying when I quit that job. And I wasn't lying when I said I'd look you up, either. I was just going to call."

"Like hell you were! You still intended to sneak off to New York."

I put my hands on her shoulders. She didn't come any closer, but she didn't back away.

"That's right, Hazel. I intended to sneak off on the fifteenth, to be exact. And I still intend to. With you."

Her eyes widened.

"But you had to spoil it for me—the whole thing could have been such a wonderful surprise. The news about the book, the way I'd planned to tell you. I meant for us to be married right away—make the trip as a honeymoon."

The way she moved in on me, you couldn't have slipped a sheet of tissue paper between us.

"Dan . . . you really mean it?"

"What do you think? Oh, darling, don't think it's been easy for me, either. I've missed you so much."

"I didn't understand. I thought——"

"Don't talk."

We spent several minutes not talking. I found other ways to be convincing. She had her head buried in my shoulder when she spoke again.

"I've never chased after a man this way before, Dan. I've got some pride, after all."

"I know you have."

"And I wouldn't have done it this time, even for you. Only——"

"Only what?"

Her words came in a rush. "You really did mean what you said, lover? About us getting married right away?"

"Of course, Hazel. You know that."

"Then I'm glad. Because, you see—I'm pretty sure now I'm going to have a baby."

It was snowing like hell outside; regular March blizzard, but I finally persuaded her we ought to go out and get drunk.

"It's our last chance," I coaxed. "Tomorrow we'll have to get a license—and tickets—and start packing. You'll be busy cleaning up your schedule here. I want to wire ahead for reservations. So it's now or never."

"But couldn't we just stay here, Dan? I'm so happy."

"If you like. But me, I feel like celebrating a little. With two brand new first editions in the family. . . ."

She giggled.

"Have a heart, Hazel. It's been a long time between drinks, and from now on you'll have to take care of yourself."

"Yes, won't I? I'm going to watch my diet and everything. Just think, Dan—I'm going to be a mother."

It was nothing to giggle about, but she did. "I suppose it'll be a red head, too."

"Are you sure you're——?"

"Two months now. Aren't you glad, darling? I am."

"I'm more than glad. I'm proud."

Yes, and I was more than proud, too. I was horrified to the point of physical nausea. I knew that unless I had a drink within the next five minutes, I'd pass out. I had to have one.

I steered her, clinging and giggling, out into the storm. In exactly four minutes by the clock, I was downing the first in a long series of double brandies.

Somewhere along the line we had supper, but I didn't pay any attention to it. It was all juke-boxes and giggling and fast, hard talking that didn't make any sense, and soft, mushy talking that did make sense in a horrible way.

We were at a place in the Loop and it was late, and she kept dancing close and rubbing up to me, whispering could I feel anything stirring yet, and the more I made her drink the more she kept talking about it.

I couldn't stop her and I couldn't stop the giggling, either, and worst of all, I couldn't stop thinking.

Then the waiter said they were closing up and then he came back and said it again in a snotty sort of way and I said "O.K." and we went someplace else where there weren't any lights and the stuff burned when it went down but it still went down.

And we were kissing in the booth and she wanted to come

back to my room but I said, "No honey you have to go home and pack," and I knew why I said it but I didn't know exactly yet.

And the juke-box was giggling and the waitress was giggling and everybody was giggling because, after all, it was such a good joke on me the smart guy, the great author, the guy who never took the rap.

Rap—that was a funny word, no wonder she giggled. It sounds like rape and then again it sounds like something else, like wrap for instance, only wrap is something you do—so is rape, only wrap is more practical; we've had our little rape so let's have a wrap and not take the rap.

Closing time . . . what the hell . . . all right . . . still blizzard, so where's the overcoat and—giggle—where's the washroom . . . right back here.

Easy boy, you can make it . . . you have to make it . . . now or never . . . there you are—oh, God something's happening . . . it can't happen—it is—hold tight—hang onto the washbowl . . . there now.

All of a sudden I was cold sober. Everything had come up and I was standing there in the men's room looking into the mirror.

Just the two of us—me and my face in the mirror—watching me button up my overcoat. Watching me wrap the maroon scarf around my neck.

Wrap. That was it!

The face in the mirror nodded at me.

I must have been thinking about it ever since she told me. All through the drunk my subconscious, or whatever it is, had been working it out; telling me to tell her she had to go home, and all the rest. That's the way it must have been. Because now I knew just what to do.

We stumbled out into the snow, with that Lake Michigan wind tearing at the skin on our cheekbones. I was cold sober—she was drunk, and hot.

She kept pulling me into doorways and kissing me, giggling. The wind ripped her giggle to shreds.

"Come on," I whispered. "We have to hurry."

It must have been almost four in the morning. We climbed up

to the El platform. It was empty. Not that you could see two feet in front of you, with the snow roaring down.

We walked to the far end, our feet crunching the snow on the boards. I saw no people. No pigeons. Just darkness and snow and wind. Just the two of us.

She shivered against me like a tired puppy. I held her close.

"Here," I said. "You're cold."

"All right, long's got you to warm me, honey. Feel."

"No, you are cold. Look, you're shivering. Wait a minute. Let me give you my scarf."

There was nobody on the platform. Nobody at all. No people-eyes. No pigeon-eyes. Just the wind, and the snow, and the dark.

I unwound the scarf from my neck and held it out.

"No. Do'needa scarf."

"Let me put it on."

"No."

I grabbed her arm and pulled her around. With my free hand I twisted the scarf.

Then she looked up at my face and she saw something there and she recognized it. She went stiff.

"Dan—no! . . . Stop!"

A rumbling cut through her words. Everything stopped, frozen, and the snow hung suspended in mid-air.

Then she pulled away and back.

I followed her, quickly. I had the scarf ready now. She turned to run.

I reached out and grabbed for her.

Missed.

Then everything speeded up.

There was a sudden glare of light behind us. It picked out her figure at the edge of the platform, silhouetted it. The rumbling swelled to a roar. An El shrieked around the curve toward the station.

The light and the noise stunned her. I almost hurled myself at her.

She recoiled. There was only one way to go—straight back, over the edge. As I reached for her, she moved.

First her face disappeared, then her arms, then her legs. The El spotlight stabbed at her body as it fell away.

Then the beam blinded me, the roar deafened me, and the El thundered down upon the station.

As I turned and ran down the steps, I thought I could hear her scream. But it was only the grinding halt of the train.

VIII

ON SUCH short notice, all I could get was an upper berth to New York, but I took it.

I had it made up as soon as I got on the train. I told the porter I was sick, and it wasn't much of a gag at that.

Lying there, feeling it get dark, I began to wonder what was ahead of me. I would meet Teffner, get close to him. The book was sold, and anything was possible from now on in. I remembered, when I was a kid, I used to dream of going back to Horton some day. Big-shot author. Well, I'd be a big shot yet, but I wouldn't go back to Horton. Or to any of those other places I'd been, including Chicago.

Especially not Chicago. Even though there was nothing to worry about. Hazel would be a plain case of suicide.

First thing, I'd write to Lou King—nice, friendly letter, telling him what I'd been doing this last month in the big town. I was pretty well covered there; everybody thought I'd left, except Hazel.

Then I'd sit back and wait for a reply from King. It would contain the news of Hazel's death. Suicide, over me.

I knew how to answer that one, too. Unless they started an investigation. But why should they investigate? The morning papers hadn't even worked up to suicide yet, and maybe they'd never even go that far. It was a straight accident story. Bad storm. El motorman's report. No witnesses. Woman slipped from platform. Hazel Hurley, 25, fashion model.

Of course, Teffner in New York knew that I'd stayed in Chicago. But chances were he'd never tell anybody. Why should he? The question just wouldn't arise—I'd see to that.

So it was all cleaned up. Even the typewriter part. I was taking it with me—when I hit town I'd express it back, with a letter. Say that I'd been called away suddenly a few weeks ago and forgot to return their machine.

Hazel had probably just phoned them for my address, so they wouldn't connect her name with mine, wouldn't even know her name. My landlady hadn't been around when she came in or when we went out.

We had gone only to strange restaurants and bars that last night and Hazel's hair had been covered by a hood, because of the storm. She'd hardly had it off the whole evening.

I went over the whole deal again and again in my mind—all but the last part. And I was clear. I knew it. There was nothing to worry about, if I didn't think of the last part.

I wouldn't think of it. I was going to New York, an author. It was silly to curl up shivering in a stuffy berth. Nerves. A good night's sleep was all I needed.

A good night's sleep. . . .

It was the fastest run I'd ever made. We pulled into Grand Central and I got out.

A porter took my typewriter and said, "You can't bring that in here," and went away with it.

The minute I got inside the waiting room I realized what he meant, because the waiting room had been fixed up like a big classroom, and you don't use a typewriter in grammar school.

It was just like Horton, and when I sat down at my desk I wasn't a bit surprised to see Miss Frazer standing up front. I always thought she was dead, but anything can happen in New York.

She smiled at me and took her glasses off the way she always did and we started our lesson on advertising. I felt funny, being in with all these kids—Beanie Harrison and Curly Mertz—and I began to pull the hair of the girl ahead of me.

I felt even funnier when the girl turned around. It was Rena, and she asked me to please stop pulling her hair and come to bed.

Miss Frazer was looking at me, so I marched right up to her and said "An apple for the teacher," and pulled one out of my pocket.

Of course it wasn't really an apple, it was Hazel's head.

But Miss Frazer just took off her glasses and said, "For that you'll stay after school young man," and winked. I winked back, knowing what she meant.

Then the bell giggled and everybody went out, and Miss Frazer locked all the doors and all the windows and all the desks and all the suitcases and all the holes in the walls that the eyes peeked through.

That was wise, because I didn't have any clothes on. She made me come up front to the blackboard and told me, "This time I'm really going to punish you for what you did. How do you ever expect to become an author if you don't write?"

She gave me a piece of chalk, very long and thick. It was red chalk and it made a mark like blood.

"Stay here until you write 'Thou shalt not kill' five hundred times on the blackboard."

So I began to write "Thou shalt not kill" on the blackboard, over and over again. This was hard, because it was getting dark and besides, she had tied up my hands.

The words began to glow like neon lights, because it was an advertising school, and I could read them in the dark. Only they had changed when I wrote them, and I read, over and over again, "Each man kills the thing he loves."

A big fat greasy man with long yellow hair simpered out and told me, "You can't write!" and I felt ashamed, because he was Oscar Wilde and he knew.

"What shall I do?" I asked, and he giggled and pointed at my chalk.

"Untie your hands. That's the secret. How can you write when Miss Frazer ties your hands?"

I looked down at my hands, and sure enough, they were still tied—with the maroon scarf.

Then I tried to get them free, working the knots down towards my wrists. But the knots wouldn't give, and the chalk made giggle-noises, and it was dark in there. I started to cry, and Oscar Wilde whispered, "Each man kills the thing he loves. Why don't you kill yourself?"

I could see then that it was the only thing to do. So I put my hands up to my neck and let the scarf flow around it, and then I was choking and choking——

*

I sat up, banging my head, as the porter bawled his way through the car.

"New York—twenty minutes!"

It had been a nice, restful sleep. I was all set for the big time, now.

But one thing I'd learned. One thing was perfectly clear; there was no alternative. I made up my mind to that. From now on—I'd have to stop killing people.

NEW YORK

IX

PHIL TEFFNER was no bigger than a dime. Everything about him was pointed—shoes, trouser creases, shoulder padding, nose, and remarks.

I was surprised to find him in a very nice layout, with eight or nine people working in a series of offices; very much like Bascomb's place.

But there the resemblance ended. The minute I gave my name I was ushered into Teffner's office. A dark-haired little dynamo pumped my arm with one hand and pressed a buzzer with the other.

"Send Pat Collins in with the Morley file," he said, into the inter-comm. Then, "Hello, Morley. Sit down and we'll go to work."

Pat Collins turned out to be Patricia—a tall, slim, sandy-haired girl in a tailored gray suit. She gave Teffner a folder and me a handshake.

"So you're Mr. Morley."

I admitted it.

"Then this belongs to you." She fished in her pocket and came out with a check.

It was Teffner's, made out to me, for nine hundred dollars.

"Your advance on the book. One thousand, minus our ten per cent."

I stifled a gulp. This was beginning to sound like the big time.

Teffner was paying no attention. He riffled through the folder, mumbling to himself.

"Ten thousand first printing, September release, maybe August, two thousand advertising and promotion, contact Kleeman, no other nibbles. Right."

I let my long-deferred gulp go through as Pat Collins turned to Teffner and stuck a cigarette between his lips. She lit it for him deftly as he continued to page through the contents of the folder.

Then both of them turned at once and faced me. I watched the cigarette balancing itself on Teffner's wobbly lower lip. An ash formed—quite a long ash.

Nobody said anything.

They kept staring at me. The ash dropped to the floor and another blossomed in its place.

"Well, what do you think?" Teffner murmured to the girl.

"I don't know. Hollis has some faith in it, if he shells out a two thousand appropriation for advertising. Or did you work on him?"

"I worked. But I'm wondering now if I worked hard enough. With Morley here, we might get them to boost the ante on the first edition. That would jack up the advertising and assure us of the reprint almost automatically."

"Perhaps."

They kept staring at me, these two, as if I were a head of cattle. Not a very choice head, either.

"Of course he'll have to get busy first of all on the revision," Teffner said, dousing the butt of the cigarette he hadn't started to smoke. "That's your department. What did Kleeman say? Does he want a lot of changes?"

"You know Kleeman," answered the girl. "I'd hate to think of what would have happened if King James had come to him with the Bible."

A buzzer sounded. Teffner rose. Pat Collins went over and stuck another cigarette between his lips. He cocked his head and she lit a match for him. He smiled at me.

"I'll have to leave you for a few moments, Morley. Meanwhile, you and Miss Collins can discuss the revision on your manuscript. She's got all the dope on it for you."

The smile froze on his lips, the cigarette tilted upwards at an antiaircraft angle, and he zipped out of the room. The door closed.

Pat Collins sat down behind the desk and thumbed at the folder. She looked at me, and I turned my head. I couldn't get that idea out of my head—I was a head of cattle to her. A bum steer.

"We have a job on our hands, Mr. Morley."

"We have?"

"Mr. Kleeman—he's in charge of editing your book at Hollis & Company—has a number of notes on suggested revisions. And he wants the manuscript in final form within six weeks, to meet publication deadlines."

"I'm ready to start."

"Fine. Perhaps if we go over his suggestions together, you'll get a better picture of what must be done."

I stepped around behind the desk and looked over her shoulder as she began to read aloud.

That next hour was one of the worst I've ever spent in my life.

Pat Collins had a Vassar voice. She read Kleeman's suggestions well—too well. I caught every implication behind the polite, carefully phrased recommendations for changes. And I knew she meant me to catch them.

The criticisms were objective. They made sense. From time to time she paused and checked certain points, indicating portions referred to in my manuscript. I didn't attempt to disagree.

How could I? Each point was obvious. And when she finished and asked, "Is everything clear?" I could only nod.

Everything was clear, all right. It was perfectly clear that my heroine, Hedy, had about as much life as a Macy window dummy. That her motivation was false. That my carefully contrived ending was out the window.

Reading between the lines, I realized that I'd made a lot of mistakes. Worse than that, I realized Kleeman knew it. Still worse, Pat Collins knew it, too.

She sat back. "Do you understand what he wants you to do?" she asked.

"Yes. I think so. He wants me to change the title to *Queen of Tarts.*"

"Please, Mr. Morley. It isn't that bad."

But it was serious, all right. You spend ten years on a milk-train en route through hell and high water to get here. And you think you've paid for your ticket with sweat and tears—yes, and with blood, too. Then you find out that you didn't arrive anywhere.

That you're right back where you started. Because you're not good enough, your work isn't good enough. You knew you could do it, you were going to show everybody you could do it—and you flopped.

How could I tell her that? A smug, smirking, frigid little college graduate, the kind that goes to concerts and art galleries with a lot of middle-aged queers and has her apartment redecorated every second year to impress the gang of Saturday night intellectuals that come up to discuss Existentialism or whatever the hell it is they happen to be misquoting at the moment—I had her pegged. Why in hell should I tell her anything? She was laughing at me, maybe she even felt sorry for me in a superior sort of way. I felt like saying, "If you're so goddamn smart, why don't you try writing a book yourself?"

She couldn't have read my mind. But she said, "Don't hesitate to ask questions. I might possibly be able to help. I've had two historical novels published, myself."

I stared at her. *She'd* had novels published! That was the last straw. I knew it, now. I didn't belong here. I'd never belong here. It wouldn't work. Now was my cue to hand back the advance check, get out of here, get out of town, run away——

Run away.

No. I couldn't run away. I'd promised myself. That would have to stop.

Somewhere I found a big smile and spread it over my face. I had trouble making it stick, but it stayed there.

"Thanks," I said. "I'm a little bit confused."

"Naturally. Discouraged, too, I imagine."

"Yes." What did I have to lose?

"It isn't so bad, you know. The revision, I mean. Those changes will strengthen the book a lot."

"And weaken me."

She lit a cigarette and nodded. "Take my word for it, you won't have any real trouble revising. Because you've got something to sell. What am I talking about—you've already sold it! You don't imagine that Mr. Teffner would be interested in you if he didn't have faith in the book. And Hollis certainly wouldn't care to risk publishing under those circumstances."

"I'm not so sure," I answered. "I've read some of those popular items he's put out. Full of sloppy sentiment, disguised by a lot of fast chatter. Fat, frustrated women turn off their serial programs to read them—skinny stenos smuggle the hot stuff under their typewriter desks."

She smiled. "Don't tell that to Mr. Hollis. You'll be meeting him in a day or so, you know."

"I didn't know."

"It's all arranged. From now on Mr. Teffner will take charge of your program. All you have to do is keep in touch with this office and follow orders. And get to work on that revision, of course."

I was surprised to find a cool hand grasping mine. She gave me another smile. "Good-by, now."

"Good-by."

She turned at the door. "Oh, just one thing more, before I forget it. I hope you won't think I'm impertinent, but I'd like to offer you a word of advice. About your habits of dress."

"Habits of dress?"

"Yes. You might find it helpful to remove that chip you're wearing on your shoulder."

She left, and Teffner scurried back into the office.

"Clever girl," he said.

"Yeah," I mumbled.

I met Stephen Hollis the following afternoon. He was a tall, tweed-bearing animal with a pipe stuck in the middle of a twisted grin. He said a few kind words about how glad he was to be associated with me in this venture, etc. I was not overly impressed and made no great effort to impress him. I was too worried about my revision.

Teffner had an in with the hotel, and I wasn't kicked out of my room. As a matter of fact, they couldn't have kicked me out—I had the place barricaded up, and I spent most of the next three weeks machine-gunning the typewriter.

This time it would have to be right. It would have to be, so I could forget Hazel. It would have to be, so no one could laugh at me—pipe-chewing publishers or cigarette-chewing agents, or pencil-chewing women. The notes helped me to turn the trick, but mostly it was sheer desperation. That's the only way I can figure it.

Point is, it worked. I turned in my revise two weeks ahead of schedule, and there was another little meeting in the Teffner agency. This time Hollis sent down a man from his publicity department, and I began to realize I was going to get quite a build up. There was talk of a big cocktail party.

"Your revision went over," Pat Collins told me, in a confidential aside. "I smell a real promotion here. From now on you're going to be a busy man, with all the plans laid for you."

"You'd better spend the next month or so getting your affairs into shape," suggested Teffner. "As we approach publication date you'll have to be prepared for a short grind. Try to find yourself a little apartment. Get settled and relax."

"Right."

"And incidentally, it isn't too early to begin planning what you're going to write next."

"Don't worry about that," I said. "I already know."

I did know.

The excitement had been a shield. The intense revision work had been a shield. The physical confinement of the hotel room had been a shield. But all shields are vulnerable.

There were chinks, cracks, interstices; every spare moment was in itself a tiny opening through which the thoughts had poured.

And now the excitement was over, the revision was over, the hotel room afforded no protection. The thoughts were coming through unchecked. Thoughts about what had happened in Chicago. Thoughts about what might still happen, if anyone ever found out about Hazel.

I went back to my place knowing what I was going to write next. I went straight to the bottom drawer of the bureau and pulled out the black notebook.

The Black Notebook

Get out your dream-books, boys.

Get out your little hammers and tap me on the knees.

Tell me about the Id and the Ego, the Psyche and the

Libido. Make it convincing. Make it good. Just so you explain why I wake up drenched with sweat. Just so you can explain a dream like this one:

It seems to me that I am lying in bed, sleep-sodden in a crummy boardinghouse room. Somewhere an alarm clock rings and I awake.

I reach over to the table next to the bed and shut off the alarm clock.

The ringing continues.

I sit up, rubbing my eyes. I glance at the table on the other side of the bed. A second alarm clock rests upon it. I shut that one off, too.

The ringing continues.

I gaze up at the bureau. You know what I see—another alarm clock. I lurch over and shut it off.

The ringing——

It seems to me the sound comes from the bathroom. I stumble in. There on the washstand is another alarm, identical with the rest. I snap it off.

But——

Suddenly I wheel and stare out the open window. Across the way looms a church steeple. In place of a regular clock-face, the huge alarm rises, complete with giant bell. It shrills in my ears as I fumble into my clothing and run wildly out of the room, through the hall and down the stairs.

I find myself at work in a large office containing many desks. I am in the corner, seated next to an older man who wears an eyeshade. He is obviously my superior in rank.

Thirsty, I eye the water cooler in the corner. I want a drink, but am afraid to get up while my older co-worker is watching.

A file girl comes by and bends over a desk. The other man leers at her rump. I take advantage of his distraction to rush over to the cooler.

Preparing to draw a drink, I notice a naked girl, about four inches long, swimming in the cooler. A miniature of Hazel, perfectly formed, alive and wriggling in the water. She looks up at me, smiling, and waves a greeting.

I attempt to draw her out of the cooler through the spout. As I do so, bubbles form at the bottom of the tank, and a six-inch silvery shape darts upward. It's a shark.

It rushes Hazel, a tiny torpedo. She flees, but the cruel mouth pursues, its razored smirk edging closer. Hazel draws a dagger from her hair and plunges it into a slitted eye. The shark closes in. A jaw opens. A jaw closes. The water is filled with red threads; a scarlet skein of death.

In a moment it's all over. Both are dead, both bodies rise to the top of the cooler and float there like goldfish.

Horrified, I turn and flee the office.

Then I climb the stairs. I come to the door marked: DOCTOR IS IN PLEASE BE SEATED. I enter.

The doctor turns out to be some kind of Hindu—at least, he wears a turban on his head.

I ask him to help me. I tell him I have a difficult problem. It calls for a good brain.

He says sure he'll help me, and he has a very good brain. To prove it, he removes his turban and shows me his brain. It looks good to me.

So we go back up to my place, because I want to show him the alarm clocks. I open the door and we go inside.

"Here they are," I say. "You see?"

I point to the table. No alarm clock. No alarm clock on the bureau, in the bathroom, over on the church.

But wherever the alarm clocks had stood before, there now rests the limp, dead-goldfish body of the red-haired girl from the water cooler. A soggy white little shape on each table, one on the bureau top, one in the bathroom. And impaled on the church steeple——

The doctor looks, shudders. His brain turns red. He rushes out, and I follow, pleading for help, for an explanation.

I stagger forth into the snow and trudge to Rockefeller Plaza. Crowds are pouring from the office buildings all around me.

Pat appears and grabs my arm.

"I must talk to you," I say. I try to tell her what has happened. She leads me into an Automat. The place is jammed. We fight our way up to the slots. I see a piece of lemon pie. I insert a dime and the door opens.

A plate emerges.

Resting on the plate is a severed human hand.

Frightened, we retreat to the swirling snow of the street. We run through the dusk, as trees loom out of nowhere. The street becomes a path, the path becomes a trail, the trail becomes a narrow opening between the boles of gigantic trees.

We enter a huge castle, dark and deserted. The vaulted room in which we stand is filled with statues of women and griffons; huge chow dogs and dragons.

Suddenly the statues close in. They move closer. They are not alive, but the pedestals move toward us, surround us.

And then they shake. The pedestals jump up and down. The faces turn to molten lava, and the chow dogs bare their fangs. The women leer. We run through an aisle of quivering stone, as the walls and windows of the castle melt and waver. The very floor churns beneath us. Everything seethes.

Then I am suddenly back in my bed in the crummy room. It's morning again, I'm all alone, and I hear the alarm clock ring.

Once again I reach over and shut it off.

It stays shut off.

"Thank God!" I mutter. "It was only a dream."

I rise, dress, and walk out of the door.

Not into the hall beyond.

Into a mouth.

Into a gigantic red mouth, gaping to fill the entire doorway. The jaws close down, the teeth rend and tear. . . .

Then I wake, really awake, and shut off the alarm clock. Then I really say, "Thank God—it was only a dream."

But one thing bothers me, even then.

Has my dream really ended? Does it ever end? And is there such a thing as a dream, after all?

X

ONE of Teffner's friends found me a small apartment within walking distance of Grant's Tomb—although that's not why I took it. Getting settled in the new place helped to take my mind off things. Reading proofs offered additional distraction.

Then, late in July, I found the build-up was on.

New clothes first. You get measured for a suit, two suits. It takes two men and a pansy to do the job. Then somebody sells you a bill of goods about having a "good address," just temporarily, and you move to an apartment on Central Park South where the doorman makes more in tips than you pay in rent.

The lady columnists with matching lipstick and toenails yawn their way through every word you've memorized in advance. The photographer, who may be a queer or just highly talented, takes two dozen pictures in a studio no bigger than a zeppelin hangar.

You read your name in a newspaper column, crediting you with a quote you never made. Meanwhile a studio station-wagon races you through the streets to an early morning breakfast broadcast, where you make bright, impromptu small-talk without rattling either your coffee cup or the script.

Insurance salesmen start ringing your phone, and the office wants you down there right away, and you're booked for a dinner date tonight, and then the suits are ready and you're getting your signals set on the cocktail party and look, here's an advance write-up on you in a book section.

You're a big-time operator.

Then you go to the cocktail party and you're nothing. I'll never be able to figure that deal out as long as I live.

Teffner and Pat called for me and drove me up to the Hollis apartment on Park Avenue. There must have been close to a hundred guests, knocking around in a living-room big enough for open bowling.

They told me later there were three pianos in the room, but I could spot only two. It was that kind of a place.

When I walked in, I was ready for anything. But I got exactly nothing.

Of course Stephen Hollis greeted me at the door, and there was a little murmur of conversation about fine early reader reaction and gratifying reports on orders. But Hollis didn't exactly twist my lapels off in his enthusiasm, and I gathered that this was all strictly routine. He addressed most of his remarks directly to Phil Teffner and Pat, and I just hovered around the edge of the group, plucking at the fringe.

I saw a couple of the press in attendance at the little portable bar, but nobody asked me for an interview or even a lock of my hair.

Finally the publicity man spotted me, charged over, and yanked me into position next to Hollis and a stylish stout I guessed must be his wife. Somebody popped a few flashbulbs and that ended that.

Meanwhile a party was going on.

A hundred people curled their tongues around olives or maraschino cherries and waited for the servants to refill their glasses. A rugged group of non-waiters stood up at the portable bar and did their own pouring.

Everybody seemed to know everybody, at least everybody who was anybody. Me, I was nobody.

And the conversation rose in waves all around me, until I went down for the third time.

". . . so why shouldn't they make a good match? He has a commercial mind and she has a commercial body . . ."

". . . something of a cross between Santayana and Danny Kaye, if you know what I mean . . ."

". . . must be a lavatory on this floor . . ."

". . . totally erroneous concept of nuclear fission . . ."

". . . you better not mess up this rug . . ."

". . . just because Hollis has a magazine running in all those languages is no sign he's running the world . . ."

". . . where is that whore-son waiter? Hey, you . . ."

". . . Verlaine, Rimbaud, Barbey d'Aurevilly, Villiers de l'Isle-Adam . . ."

". . . at Meadowbrook, Sunday. But if he finds out, I'll have to phone you in the afternoon . . ."

"... a complete chain-reaction is impossible. Look at the de Sitter formulae and you'll realize that..."

"... Octave Mirbeau, the de Goncourts, even poor Louis-Ferdinand Celine..."

"... Christ, I can't hold it any longer..."

Then Pat was beckoning to me, and a tall, brown-haired woman with a mannish haircut held out her hand. There happened to be a drink in it, so I took it.

"Constance Ruppert ... Daniel Morley, our celebrity," said Pat.

"I've seen your photograph," said Constance Ruppert, in a husky voice. "It didn't do you justice."

She looked at me. I looked at her hair, which was the color of Swiss chocolate. She brushed it back, and I caught the glare of an exploding universe from the diamond on her little finger.

"So you're an authority on women," said the soft voice.

I had an answer for that one, but I didn't know her well enough to pull it.

"But haven't I seen you somewhere before, Mr. Morley?"

"Not that I know of." Women with diamonds that big I don't forget.

She wrinkled her forehead and pouted. Her everted lips were moist and soft. "I'm quite positive we've met. I have an exceptional memory for faces, particularly if they're handsome ones."

Mine made a handsome smirk. "You must be mistaken. You see, I'm from out of town."

"That's just it," said Constance Ruppert. "I don't connect you with New York. Could you possibly have been in Chicago? I visited there around the middle of March."

The smirk froze suddenly. "No. I was in Chicago early this year, but I left there in February."

"Strange." She gave a soft chuckle. "Well, it doesn't matter. The important thing is that we've finally met. But I can't help feeling we're really old acquaintances."

"Good. I need a few friends in a mob like this."

She glanced around the room and nodded. "I see what you mean. This is pretty deadly, isn't it? Standing around drinking and talking until they fall down. And some of them go right on drinking and talking on the floor."

"The drinking I can understand. It's the talking that's so difficult."

Constance Ruppert patted my shoulder. Her touch, like her voice, was surprisingly soft. "What you need, my dear boy, is somebody to show you the ropes."

So that's what they called it here. I must remember the line. How would you like to come up to my apartment and see my collection of ropes? I'll tie a few Boy Scout knots for you—show you the old Hindu rope trick. . . .

"But I want to hear something about your book. Everybody seems to think it's bound to be a great success. I know Hollis is rushing it through so it will appear early on the Fall list."

She didn't have to keep patting my shoulder that way. The touch and voice were still soft, but there was something about her eyes I didn't quite like.

"You know, you don't even sound like an author. Most of them talk about themselves all the time. And you hardly talk at all."

"Need another drink, I suppose." I started to move away.

"Oh, let me get it for you. After all, we're old friends—since we nearly met in Chicago."

There it was again. Now I knew what I didn't like about her eyes. That half-look of recognition. She was still trying to remember me.

I glanced around warily, then repressed a sigh of relief as I caught sight of Pat Collins heading my way again. She had somebody else in tow—a tall, rangy-looking man with a crew haircut. Probably a college boy turned reporter.

"Here you are," she sang out. "I've got somebody who wants to meet you."

"Is there such a person?"

"Daniel Morley . . . Jeffrey Ruppert."

"Jeff, darling this is a surprise!" Constance Ruppert was patting *his* shoulder now. He didn't look any happier about it than I had.

"You two related?" I asked.

"By marriage," Constance said. "He happens to be a former husband of mine, and a very nice one."

Probably he divorced her before she could wear out the shoulder-padding in all his suits.

"I understand you're being groomed as the next expert on feminine psychology," said Ruppert.

"Pay no attention to him," Pat interposed, taking his arm. I noticed she maneuvered him carefully out of range of the patting. "Jeff's a psychoanalyst himself. You've read *Penny for Your Thoughts,* haven't you?"

"Oh, you're *that* Ruppert?" I was genuinely surprised. His book had been a minor best-seller last season; come to think of it, Hollis had published the volume.

"Guilty," Ruppert answered, fumbling with a pipe.

"But I always thought you must be an older man."

"Hard to judge a man by his writing," said Ruppert, seriously. "Actually, it's only a pot-boiler. The popular approach. But it seems that in our decadent society one must adopt accepted techniques in order to get a hearing."

"I want you two to have a talk sometime," Pat told me. "But this is neither the time nor the place for it."

"Certainly not," said Constance, quickly. "After all, we're supposed to be at a party—not a clinic."

Ruppert nodded. "I'll be seeing you again, Morley."

He moved away, and I noticed that Pat was working his arm now.

Constance Ruppert turned to me with another pout. "Don't let him fool you. He probably wants to pump you on what you know about feminine psychology. The poor dear is very deficient in that department, take it from one who knows."

"You don't like him, do you?"

"Oh, Jeff's terribly clever—he looks like a boy, but he's really a genius, I suppose, in his own field. After all, he did do wonders for me."

"You?"

"Yes. I was a patient of his before we were married. As a psychoanalyst, he's remarkably competent. As a husband——" The pout expanded.

We approached the bar. A white-sleeved arm proffered Manhattans.

Constance Ruppert twirled her glass until the cherry bobbed. She stared at it. Then she stared at me.

"Red," she said. "Isn't that silly of me? I *still* think I've seen you somewhere before. And I seem to associate you with the color red. Red something—hair, or a necktie, or a scarf——"

I stared at the cherry. All at once I knew I had to do something. Run out of the room, run away from this woman. To hell with her, to hell with the party, to hell with the book. Run.

Only I wasn't going to run any more. There had to be another way to stop her, another way to divert her attention, check her attempts at complete recollection.

All at once I found myself talking, loud and fast. Pat was there, and Ruppert, and Hollis, and all the rest. My voice got louder, and I talked faster and faster.

"That cherry," I said. "I suppose your husband would call it an example of simple association. I'm not overly familiar with all the current labels in psychoanalysis. But the labels aren't important—they're still selling the same old package. Skull oil for an aching brain."

"You don't approve of psychoanalysis or psychiatry?"

That's how I knew Jeff Ruppert was there.

"I don't object to the methods—the aims are at fault."

"Aims?"

"As near as I can figure it out, the object of psychoanalysis is to get people to make adjustments so they can live normally. And that's wrong."

He was listening now. Most of them were listening. But I didn't give a damn whether they listened or not, just as long as I could keep talking, keep stalling.

"My experience is that abnormality pays off. Wait a minute, now—I'm not going to drag out those trite examples of writers, or painters, musicians and entertainers—or psychoanalysts, either. We all know they're crazy.

"I'm speaking of the so-called common herd. The ones you generally accept as being fairly adjusted. Well, they're not. I know, because I'm one of them and I've lived with them all my life.

"Take a good look at the man in the street, the man in the bus, the man in the upper flat. Mr. Average Citizen, Mr. Voter, Mr. Taxpayer—hang any label you choose to around his neck. He's still maladjusted.

"The bum salesman who lives off his wife, the hypochondriac woman who makes her kids slave for her, the nagging bitch whose husband is tied to her apron strings, the crotchety older relative with money and a religious fixation, the smart-aleck good-looking boy whose doting parents pull him out of everything from a scrape to a rape. There's one in every family. And somehow they all get along.

"That's the important part, don't you see? They get along in spite of everything. And meanwhile the 'normal' people—the ones willing to take the rap, work like hell humoring the so-called misfits and repairing the damage they've done—it's the 'normal' people who are unhappy, who worry, brood, feel guilty, hide their troubles and fears and desires. Call it sublimation or compensation, tag it any way you like. If psychoanalysis and psychiatry will be used to effect such a 'normal' outlook, then I say the aims are all wrong."

"Then you believe maladjustment is the key to success?" asked Stephen Hollis, quickly.

"Who's talking about success? I'm talking about happiness. And that's another thing. It ties right in with our little psychoanalytical problem.

"You, all of you here, are success-conscious. You write and preach and sell success all day long, and at night you worship it in your dreams. But that's a mistake.

"Too many people are training for success. We ought to spend our time training more failures.

"Every economic survey, every census, shows the truth. Very few people can become successful, in the sense of the word you accept. Large numbers inevitably fail.

"So why not prepare people for failure? To hell with schools and churches and books and magazines and movies with their rags-to-riches formula. Why not condition people to the truth?

"There's a real goal for psychiatry and psychoanalysis. Learn how to turn out more satisfied failures! We'd have less discontent, less idleness, less wasted effort—and above all, we'd have a variety of goals in life instead of just one stupid lie as a standard.

"Look around, that's all I ask you. We're living in a nation of failures—grasping men and frustrated women, discontented youth and grumbling oldsters.

"Better still, look around this room, at the self-acknowledged successes. Look at each other!

"Popular publishers and popular agents and popular authors, meeting with representatives of popular newspapers and magazines, and indulging in the popular pastimes of a Bowery tavern—getting blind drunk, making cheap assignations, knifing each other in the back. You're no better than the rest, no happier. It's still anything to make a dollar, an impression, or a woman."

The red was fading now. I saw nothing but eyes, staring at me. I blinked and moved away.

"I didn't think this was going to turn into a sermon," I said, slowly edging toward the door. "All I can say is, if I've done anything to mar the success of this party, I'm glad."

I ran down the hall, out the door. It was sunset in the streets.

XI

"I'LL never forget it!" said Teffner. "Did you see the look on their faces?" He began to laugh, and the cigarette dropped out of his mouth. Pat went over and inserted a fresh one.

"But Morley here gets away with it. That I still can't figure out. Everybody's buzzing over that blowoff of his. I got five calls today, complimenting me."

He came over and poked my shoulder. "Got to hand it to you, Dan. You had that gang pinned to the ropes. Connie Ruppert couldn't get over it. You seem to have made a big hit with her."

"And that's important," Pat chimed in. "You see, she actually owns about half the firm. Inherited it from her father. She and Hollis will really push the book now."

"For once I've got something to work on," the publicity man exulted. "A character. Plenty of color." He started a little pacing act of his own. I wondered how often Teffner had to replace his carpets.

"A smart job, all right. I used to do ghost writing. I know what it is to turn out a speech that won't offend anyone. But you managed to steer clear of Communism and religion and politics and still tell 'em off. We'll stick to that gimmick from now on."

Apparently I had done something clever. All I knew was that everything was rosy again.

"Well, time to run along." The public relations man scurried toward the door like a rat on a chunk of ice. He smiled benignly. "With Hollis boosting the print order, I'll have to get busy in a hurry. I'll want more information from you later, Morley. Coming with me, Phil?"

"Right along." Teffner rose and followed the publicity man from the room. I was alone with Pat.

I leaned back and pulled out a cigarette. Apparently her contract called for servicing only Teffner.

"How do you feel about all this?" she asked. "You look pretty bad, you know."

I don't like overly observant women.

"Just tired, I suppose. Things are happening too fast for me."

"I was sorry for you yesterday."

"Sorry? For me?"

"Yes. I could see how frightened you were. You *were* frightened?"

I paused, then grinned. "Scared stiff. But how did you know?"

"I didn't. At least, I wasn't quite sure of it. But I talked things over with Jeff after the affair, and he told me that in his opinion there was no doubt about it."

I couldn't keep the scowl from showing, at least around the edges. "Ruppert, eh? You mean the boy psychoanalyst?"

I hadn't meant to make it sound that way, but she froze. "Don't belittle Jeff Ruppert, just because he's got your number. He knows why you made such a scene. Because you were afraid, because you wanted to run away. Because you know your book is a fake, and you're a fake; you don't really belong."

"You really think that of me?"

"Well." She turned her head and faced the window as she

spoke. It was open, and the breeze churned the curls on her neck. "I'm just telling you what Jeff said. He's the analyst. And you were afraid."

"All right, Pat. I was afraid. And why shouldn't I be? Look, I want you to know this, because I've got a feeling you can understand.

"When I was eighteen, I ran away from home. Never finished school. Never went back. For almost ten years I was on my own. Call me a bum, if you like. Did odd jobs. I've been in jail. Everything came the hard way.

"It does something to you, Pat. Gives you what your friend Ruppert would call an inferiority complex. And at the same time, you learn to cover it up. To talk fast, crack wise, pretend you're all right, everything's all right. But you know it's wrong.

"Sometimes you get away with it. I learned how to do that pretty well. I can pull a bluff. Maybe Ruppert is right—maybe I'm pulling a bluff now, pretending to be a writer, pretending to mix in with the big-timers.

"But there's more to it than just that. You see, I've worked hard to get here. Learning to read with a purpose, learning to analyze, learning to write—all tough jobs when you're carrying the banner. Well, I made it. Or I tried to make it. And I wrote this book.

"I figured maybe it would pull me out of everything; the dirty flops, the greasy kitchens, the damp boxcars, the grimy streets, sour taverns, cheap hotels. It's my big chance. I'll probably never get another.

"So you start giving me a fast build-up, you turn the lights on me, shove me in with that crowd of smart operators. Of course I'm scared. Wouldn't you be?"

Pat turned around. She wasn't sneering and she wasn't smiling. She was looking at me. Just looking. Like it was the first time she'd ever seen me.

"Yes," she said. "I'd be scared. Only I'd never be in such a spot. You see, I couldn't take that hard way up, and I couldn't have the confidence to pull a successful bluff. All I can do is sit back smugly and pick on a guy who had the guts to do the job. And I'm such a heel I don't even know how to apologize decently."

"I know one way," I said.

"Such as?"

"Such as having lunch with me this noon."

She shook her head. "Sorry, pal. That's out."

"Another date?"

"I'm afraid so."

"Dr. Ruppert, isn't it?"

"Yes."

"I see."

There was an awkward silence. The breeze mingled cigarette smoke with her hair.

"We're going to be married next year—he's setting up practice with his father in California."

I nodded. I wasn't really interested. I was tired. I just wanted to sit here and watch the wind play in a girl's hair while she talked to me.

The phone rang. Pat picked it up and answered. Then she frowned and handed it to me.

"Call for you," she said.

"But nobody knows I'm here——"

I took the phone.

A soft voice sounded.

"Mr. Morley? This is Constance Ruppert."

I'd had a hunch. . . .

"I took the liberty of finding out if you might be in Phil's office this morning. I would like very much to discuss promotion on your book, and I was wondering if you'd be free for luncheon?"

I said certainly I was free and where was I to meet her?

"I'll pick you up in a half hour."

"Right."

Pat looked at me and bit her lip.

"Constance Ruppert," I said.

"I know. She wants to have lunch with you, doesn't she?"

"Why not?"

"That's a long story. I'd rather Jeff told you. He probably will, if I ask him to. But, Dan—be careful with that woman. She's bad medicine."

"Don't worry your pretty head about me, dear," I said. "I'm not afraid any more."

But I was.

The Black Notebook

I open the notebook and take up the pen, and here I am, playing with words again. Even in crisis and despair, I play with words. Why not? Crisis . . . despair—they're words, too.

Words. Actions speak louder. Or do they? Not any more. Literacy has changed that. It's all words now.

You learn to speak as a child, learn to read. If you don't speak and read correctly, you're shamed. You find out the importance of words by the time you're six.

After years of this, you learn to worship words. Words like, "I pledge allegiance, Scout's Honor, Our Father Who Art in Heaven." Mystic syllables with strange powers, ruling the world.

Words that rule nations. Words that sentence men to death. Words called Laws.

A jumble of words on a slip and a mumble of words on a lip and you're married. Or divorced. Or buried, for that matter. You can't buy, sell, or contract without a magic formula. It's all words now.

So you get sick of these kinds of words and you read books—letting other words enchant you and release you from the bondage of more familiar words. But you only end up by exchanging one kind of word-slavery for another.

There are words for this dilemma, too. Psychology has a lot of words. Psychology says, in great big polysyllables, "Go out and meet people." You meet them and you talk. Say the right words and they answer in kind with other words. Say the wrong ones and they get angry.

It's confusing. So you go to philosophy and discover men seeking the secret of life by explaining all words and systems of words with other words. Talking about words with words. Using semantics.

No, you can't get behind the words, try as you may. You

can't touch the real mystery. You walk along, thinking about it, with your head bent. A man with his head bent—a walking question mark.

Words in books, magazines, newspapers. Words writhing in neon. Words crawling across billboards and window glass. Words screaming from placards. Words stamped on the sides of matchboxes and skyscrapers alike. Words blatting from the radio. Words scrawled on fence posts, car doors, sidewalks. Words trailing from airplanes in the sky.

Do this. Don't do that. Buy so and so. Believe thusly. Words will cure your headache, words will pep you up, words will give you health, wealth, popularity, beauty, happiness, heaven, and a hot loving from the most beautiful girl in the world. Words are Liberty, Equality, Fraternity, Home, Mother, Love, Hate, Vitamins, God.

Die for them. Listen to words if you can't see them, listen to the voices—the orators, your elders, the wise old business man, the politician, the preacher. Get your words today, mister. Get 'em from your friends. Can't live without words. Give us this day our daily bread.

You talk like this, people will say you're going crazy. There are even separate words for the kinds of craziness, and they'll tell you which kind yours is. You're a big word yourself.

Only deep down inside, there's a "you" who doesn't need words, can't use them. A "you" that cannot talk to others, has no communication. And you try so hard to get through to the others, but it's no use. . . .

The other night, taking that walk, I tried to think about that. But all I got was "word-pictures." I walked along and the words came between me and the thoughts.

The moon showed the curved sidewalk as the back of a white snake on which I trod. A white worm, perhaps. Worms to eat the tongue that speaks the word. When you forget words, you're dead. Like Pontius Pilate. He's a word, now. Once he lived, now he's a word on a history page, a word in the warm, red, fungus-breeding cavity of a mouth.

Many others lived and died, but did not become enduring words. Pilate was lucky. He became a word because he asked a question: "What is Truth?"

I know the answer. "Truth is . . . a word."

But I don't know the answer to the one word that really bothers me. That big word.

Murder.

That's the word I can't explain, can't understand.

Maybe this is the answer, the real answer. That murder isn't a word. It never is, never was, never will be a word like all the rest.

Murder isn't manslaughter, justifiable homicide, self-defense, mercy killing, lynching, war, accidental death. These are words, but they don't mean a thing.

Murder is something you do. Something the real you feels, experiences, lives by, lives with. That's the only way I can put it, in *words.*

There's only one way to learn the truth, and that's through action.

Murder isn't a word. Murder is a deed.

XII

I WAS pretty busy for about a week, and that was good, because as a result I slept soundly, without dreams. I wanted to see my notebook filled up with story ideas, not nightmares.

Teffner called me in, all excited over a possible deal with R.K.O. on the book, but it fell through. As a consolation prize, he handed me another check for advance royalties, on the strength of the doubled first printing.

Any way I looked at it, I was sitting pretty, and he started to needle me about doing some more short yarns.

"It isn't too early to begin thinking about your next book, either," he told me. "You're having a run of luck. Most writers would have to work years for the kind of breaks you've been getting. Why, you've never even had a rejection. And your revision work was nothing compared to what some of the boys go through. Might as well keep going. You're sitting on top of the world."

I was sitting there, but not alone. I began to discover that it would take more than the Thomas Scalp people to keep Constance Ruppert out of my hair.

She called me for lunch. She called me for dinner. She wore high-necked gowns. She wore low-necked gowns. She leaned over me. She leaned back. She gave me a royal pain.

But there was no escaping her.

Maybe if she hadn't had that idea about remembering me from Chicago, things might have worked out better. And then again, maybe not.

Of course, Teffner was pleased as hell.

"Play up to her," he kept telling me. "She knows all the right people. She can swing a lot of weight around here."

I told Teffner where she could swing her weight, but I went on seeing her. There was nothing else to do.

And then it was August 10 and the book came out, with reviews and window displays—the works. By this time I was in it thick enough to be able to talk about "distribution" and all the rest of it in a bored voice, but I was pretty excited, way down inside.

"*Queen of Hearts* by Daniel Morley" screamed out from the jacket with its heart-shaped design and a blonde girl's head featured. I turned it over, counted the pages, read the blurb and the little puff about myself on the back. I looked at it in the windows downtown.

I was pretty happy that day. I felt like celebrating, and told Pat so when I dropped up to the office.

"Nothing elaborate—just a nice quiet dinner someplace. Maybe down in the Village," I suggested.

"I'd like to. But you've forgotten the party."

"What party?"

"Constance Ruppert is throwing a brawl for you. I thought you knew—or is it supposed to be a surprise?"

"First I'd heard of anything."

"Sorry. Guess it was a surprise, after all. Be a good boy and act surprised anyway, will you?"

"All right. So I'll act surprised."

What there was to be surprised about I don't know. The party was held in her white-tiled suite, which for some reason always reminded me of an overgrown bathroom with a lot of furniture.

The usual crowd was there: Hollis, his wife, Teffner, Teffner's current girl friend, Jeff Ruppert and Pat, two other couples, and myself.

The usual congratulations were offered, and the usual drinking began. Constance had a colored maid who served and kept changing the records on the big Capehart. It was very dull.

I was beginning to find out that I'd been right when I told off these people that day at Hollis's place. They weren't particularly happy, and they didn't know how to go about having a good time.

I knew them well enough by now to detect little undercurrents of distrust, jealousy, suspicion. Mrs. Hollis hated Phil Teffner because he was "loud" and "vulgar." Constance disliked Pat because she was Jeff Ruppert's girl. Pat didn't think much of Stephen Hollis. And I hated Ruppert.

I'd never gotten back at him for his little analysis of my conduct at the first party. But it still rankled. I had the feeling that he was always watching me, studying, analyzing. That was bad.

Because of that, and because I was bored stiff, I began to drink. I hadn't been hitting the sauce all summer because of work, and the need for watching myself around Constance.

Tonight I got that what-the-hell feeling and took on a load of Scotch. It didn't particularly mellow me, but I felt more at ease, less conscious of the restlessness that crackled like heat lightning across the room.

Then, all at once, I was sitting on the sofa in the corner and Jeff Ruppert loomed up before me. He was tall and lanky, and somebody had just gone over his crew haircut with a lawnmower, making him look more like a college boy than ever.

"Mind if I sit down?" he asked.

"Come right in, the Scotch is fine," I said.

"Been wanting to have a talk with you, Dan, ever since Pat let me read the page proofs on your book."

That was mighty sweet of the girl, I thought. I also thought that I'd like to break her neck.

"If you're searching around for a delicate way in which to tell me it stinks, don't bother," I said.

Ruppert chuckled and pulled out his pipe. He filled it carefully, as if he were using opium.

"You're a bit on the defensive tonight, aren't you?"

"A brilliant analysis, Doctor. But after all, that book's my first baby. It may be a homely little bastard, but I love it."

His chuckle got mixed up inside the pipe somewhere, and a gurgle came out.

"You needn't worry, Dan. I like your book. It surprised me."

He was looking right at me, and I could see he meant it. Either that, or he had a damned good bedside manner.

"Frankly, I didn't expect to enjoy it. The plot, the treatment, was pretty run-of-the-mill stuff. But your women . . . !"

He pointed his pipe at me.

"You know a lot about women, don't you, Dan?"

"I'm over twenty-one, if that's what you mean."

"That isn't what I mean, and you realize it. I'm serious, Dan. You write about women objectively, and that's rare in contemporary literature. You catch their mannerisms, their speech rhythms, accurately, on a variety of cultural levels. Your evaluations are obviously the work of a trained observer."

"I guess we all try to figure out what makes them tick."

"You needn't be coy, Dan. This interests me greatly. I'd like to understand how you achieved your insight. Perhaps you're not aware of just what you've done. But you have a genuine talent, an insight worth cultivating. You can do things with it, Dan."

He wasn't trying to snoop. I could feel his sincerity. Maybe he wasn't such a bad guy at that—after all, he'd only told the truth about me. Besides, I was drinking a lot of Scotch. So all at once I found myself telling him.

"It's this way, Jeff. I've made my living off women."

He smiled, puffing on his pipe.

"Ever since I can remember it's been that way. My aunts used to make a big fuss over me when I was a kid. Gave me everything I wanted. Stuck up for me when my old man wanted to whale me. In school the teachers went out of their way to be nice.

"I guess I resented it, at first. I was sort of a good-looking kid, and the gang razzed me about it. For a long time, after I ran away, I didn't have anything to do with women.

"I can't ever remember having a steady girl friend. Of course, the life I was leading, you just don't get many chances. And I had no money for whores."

The Capehart was playing Stravinsky, and somebody was laughing in a voice like a fingernail ripping a bedsheet, and talk bounced off the tiles all around me. But Ruppert refilled his pipe and I went on:

"Then, somewhere along the way, I found out that I didn't need any money.

"I found out that it didn't matter if my clothes were no good and I needed a shave. One look at my collar-ad profile and the housewives gave me a handout. Sometimes more than a handout.

"I won't fool you, Ruppert. With what I had, I could have turned pimp any time. I began to study up a little, analyze my approach. I learned a boyish, appealing smile, and a line of talk to go with it. Eventually, I put it to work for me.

"Women got me every break I've ever had. My first job, back in Chicago. And now——"

That was the wrong thing to say, and I stopped. But Ruppert was way ahead of me.

"Now there's Constance," he finished, for me. "I understand."

"But I'm not pulling that stuff with Constance. It's just——"

"I know that, too. She's after you." Ruppert grinned at me. "After all, I was married to the woman. You needn't feel self-conscious." His grin faded as he leaned forward.

"But there's one thing I'm curious about, Dan. With all your perception of the feminine mind, why do you hate women?"

I didn't have any answers ready for that one.

He leaned closer. "You don't happen to be a homosexual, do you?"

Guys get hit for saying things like that, but somehow he asked the question honestly, the way a doctor would.

"No. Quite the contrary."

"But you do hate women."

"How do you figure that?"

"I don't figure. It's there, in the book. More than detachment, cynicism, objectivity—I can sense pure hatred in your descriptions and the attitudes behind them. Actually, you don't describe. You dissect. Sadistically."

"Wait a minute, now, I'm not Jack the Ripper."

"Are you sure?"

Once again he had me off balance.

"Are you positive that you aren't writing as a sort of safety valve, to keep you from taking more direct action?"

"Are you positive you aren't trying to psychoanalyze me?"

Ruppert sat back and shrugged. "Maybe so. I think you'd make a very interesting patient, Dan."

"Who's a patient?" Connie, to the rescue. For once I was glad to see her.

"I am," I told her. "I was hoping that Jeff would prescribe another drink."

"You win," said Ruppert. "But I'd still like to talk it over with you again."

Constance led the way to the bar. Ruppert lagged behind long enough to murmur in my ear. "Remind me to talk to you about my ex-wife, too."

"What's up?"

"Nothing much. Except that I've got a pretty good hunch she may try to kill you."

Then Pat took over and I didn't get a chance to talk to Ruppert again. I wanted to ask what he meant by that wild statement. Teffner and Hollis cornered me immediately. Ordinarily, I'd have played up to Hollis, but not now. Ruppert's parting remark kept buzzing around in my brain.

Maybe he was crazy. Maybe Constance was crazy. Maybe I was crazy.

I took a drink on each possibility.

Then, just as the party started getting rough, it suddenly broke up. Everybody went home.

The maid disappeared, and Constance stood there in the midst of the half-filled glasses and heaped ash trays.

I looked for my hat.

"Thanks," I said. "It was a swell party."

Constance picked up the broken end of a swizzle stick and shook her head.

"Don't kid me," she said. "It was perfectly foul."

I stole her act and patted her shoulder.

"You're just tired."

"Of course I'm tired, Dan. Tired of watching those god-awful bores. Here I meant to have a little celebration for you, and everything went wrong. Why, I didn't even get a decent chance to see you all evening."

"I was around."

"Talking to Jeff." She pulled me down alongside her on the sofa and stared at me. "I saw you two in a huddle. Tell me, what's that ex-husband of mine up to now? Trying to make trouble again?"

"No trouble. We were discussing my book. He said some mighty pretty things."

Constance leaned forward. A bottle of Scotch and a siphon stood conveniently at hand on a coffee-table. She did a professional job of mixing.

"Don't trust that man, Dan."

The drink was strong. It tightened my instep.

"Why not?"

"He's a louse. Never trust a man who doesn't trust you. Oh—forget about it. Let's have another drink."

I started to shake my head, but she was already pouring. And this shot began to curl inside me.

"This is nice, Dan. I can talk to you. You'll never know what a relief it is, just talking to somebody—not having to worry that every word you say is being put under a microscope, weighed, tested, analyzed."

"Jeff, eh?"

"He's clever, Dan. Wicked and clever. I was just a little fool when I met him. I didn't know. I was frightfully nervous and sensitive in college. My father sent me to see Jeff when I left in mid-term of the last year.

"At first I thought Jeff was wonderful; so gentle and patient. So kind. I never had much kindness, you know."

She sucked intently at the rim of her glass.

"So he told you I was his patient, did he? Did he tell you that he married me for my money? Because he wanted social prestige, a wealthy practice?"

This time I mixed the drinks.

"Did he tell you how he tried to take over after my father died? How he wanted to get his hands on the estate, push me out?"

She began to pant a little.

"Did he tell you how he worked his little campaign—choosing my friends, prescribing for me, ordering my life? All for my own good, you understand, because I wasn't well. Did he tell you that he was trying to drive me insane?"

She grabbed my arm, but not to pat it.

"Did he tell you that? About the way he frightened me, describing what he said were my symptoms, whispering to all my friends—"

Suddenly she broke off with a laugh. It wasn't the kind of a laugh you like to hear coming from a woman.

"But of course he didn't! Not good old Jeff! Not that simple, unassuming nice guy with the crew haircut that fools people into taking him for a kid. He wouldn't tell you that! Because he's too clever."

She leaned over me, snarling deep in her throat like a cougar.

"Only he wasn't clever enough for me, do you hear? I got my divorce. And when my lawyers finished with him, he had no reputation left, and no practice, either."

I could smell the whisky and the perfume coming off her, and something else. She gritted her teeth.

"Why doesn't he go to the Coast the way he says he will? What's he hanging around for? Waiting for that woman, I suppose—the new one—Pat."

The laugh knifed again in my ear. I stared deep into her eyes.

"You don't like it when I mention her name, do you, Dan? Because you want her, too. I know. I can see it. Well, you won't have her. Jeff's got his hooks into her and she's lost. And it serves her right. After all, she's just another sweet-faced, foul-minded, smug little bitch!"

I hit her across the mouth.

It hung open, a big red circle. A gasp came out of it, then a little trickle of blood.

Her fingers dug into my arms. Her eyes were all whites.

"She's a bitch, Dan. Do you hear me? A bitch—a bitch——"

I hit her again.

Then I pushed her back on the couch. Very slowly, methodically, I began to rip her dress, while her laugh screamed in my ears.

XIII

THE moment I hit Constance in the face, I knew I was in love with Pat Collins.

That's all, brother. There's nothing more to say. The only thing you can say about a thing like that is words—second-hand words, soiled words, words that have been kicked around so long in cheap songs and bad dialogue that they don't mean a thing.

Or they do mean something, but not the way you really feel. So I'll let it alone.

I loved her.

She wasn't too pretty, and she wasn't even built right; she had a sharp tongue, and she didn't like me, much. Besides, she was marrying Jeff Ruppert.

But there it was.

I'd never been in love before, not that way. The way it hurts.

For the first time, I began to realize the way Hazel Hurley might have felt; even Rena had a taste of it, I suppose. And now Constance, in her own way. . . .

But I didn't want to think about Constance. I didn't want to get into a rut with her. And rut is the right word.

I wanted Pat. And I couldn't have her. Or could I?

She was sitting in the office when I came in. The Venetian blinds were half-open, the sunlight striping her hair. I noticed how long her eyelashes were. She had the skin for freckles, but no freckles. When she smiled, her nose twitched. . . .

"Hello, Dan. Where've you been keeping yourself?"

"Out of trouble."

My voice was husky, and it wasn't all hangover.

"Clipping service is sending in reviews. You've got a good press, Dan."

"That's fine." What the hell did I care about my reviews? The inside of her arm, at the elbow, was the whitest spot in the world. . . .

"Looking for Phil? He's out with a friend from out-of-town. Should be back soon."

"I'll wait." I sat down. She kept on reading letters. The little vein in her wrist was purple. . . .

"Pat."

"Yes?"

"Pat, what do you think of me?"

She looked up and put the letters down. Her eyes had little flecks, tawny flecks. . . .

"Why, you're doing great, pal. It wouldn't surprise me to hear that Hollis will run another twenty thousand in a week or so."

"No, Pat. That isn't what I mean. What do you think of me, personally."

"You're a nice guy. I'm beginning to admire you for the way you're taking all this. We get some pretty phony characters in the agency business. And you've certainly hit it off well enough with everyone I've talked to—particularly Constance Ruppert."

"Never mind Constance Ruppert. There's only one person whose opinion means a damn to me, and that's you."

"What's all this for, Dan? I don't follow you."

"Well, follow this." I got up and stood over her. My shadow darkened the V of her neck. . . .

"Pat, I'm in love with you. I want you to marry me, now."

She gave me a long look—the same as that day when I'd rattled off my song-and-dance about my hard life.

"You—you really mean it, don't you?"

I didn't answer. She could see my face.

"Dan, I don't know what to say. I don't. Can't you see that Jeff and I are——"

"Listen, Pat. You've known Ruppert a long time. He's had all the breaks. He's taken you out, showed you a good time, pitched a line. I understand. And maybe I'm moving a little too fast for you, and it's a mistake. All I ask, then, is the same chance Ruppert had. To see you, take you out, give you a chance to get to know me.

"Then you can decide for yourself, about both of us. That's the fair way, isn't it? Why not give me a chance, give yourself a chance? I love you enough to want to see you happy, no matter how it turns out for me. I'll be satisfied either way. Because I want you, Pat. I need you."

Even with a violin it wouldn't have been any good.

"I can't, Dan. I love Jeff, and I know it. That's the way it is."

That's the way it is. . . .

That's the way it is when the Doctor says "Cancer." The way it is when the judge says, "And may God have mercy on your soul." The way it is when you scream for help, and all you can hear is the dark water rising all around you, the flames roaring in your ears. . . .

"I'm sorry, Dan."

"That's all right," I told her. "That's the way it is."

From what Constance had told me, I expected Jeff Ruppert's office to be a hole in the wall. It turned out that he had a very nice setup; soft lights, usual Chinese prints on the reception-room walls, and a secretary pretty enough to play nurse in a blackout sketch.

About a minute after I gave my name, Ruppert came striding out of his office.

"Dan, good to see you!" He had that old college grip, all right. "Come in. When is my next appointment, Miss Lee?"

She told him three o'clock, Doctor.

"Fine. That gives us plenty of time for a visit. Or did you come here for a professional consultation?"

I wasn't going to tell him why I'd come here, so I said it was just a visit.

Inside, he had an office furnished like a living room. No desk, no cabinets, no instruments. Just chairs and a couch, and a lot of lamps.

I grinned at the couch. "The old psychoanalytical routine, eh, Jeff? Lie right down and relax while I probe your psyche."

"You don't take my profession too seriously, do you, Dan?"

"On the contrary. That's why I'm here, because I value your insight."

"How can I help you?" He sat in the leather armchair and I took the couch. "Cigarette?"

"Thanks." He began his non-union plumber's routine with a pipe.

"The other night, you said something that disturbed me."

He nodded. "Constance."

"Right. Frankly, I'm beginning to find myself a bit—emotionally involved." I looked away. "Of course, I realize the whole matter is a bit delicate. Professional confidences, and the fact that she was your wife and is now——"

"Your mistress." He nodded again. A spark fell out of his pipe. "Oh, you needn't worry on that score. Your worries might begin if such were not the case." He stepped on the spark. "That's what I meant when I said she might attempt to kill you. If you resisted her . . . advances."

"What are you driving at?"

"Constance is a nympholept."

"You mean, oversexed?"

"More than that. Nympholepsy is much more than a mere physical condition; a glandular maladjustment may, however, be a contributory cause. In the old days they called the condition 'nymphomania.' It's probably a better term. Because a woman so afflicted is a maniac."

I put out my cigarette. My mouth was too dry.

"Insatiable sexual appetite is a terrible thing, Dan." Somehow Ruppert didn't sound like a college boy any more. "It rarely appears in its pure form, however. Often it is accompanied by delusions, hallucinations. You've surely heard the old legends about the incubus: the carnal night demon who visits women in their dreams. Witches had such delusions—and nuns, too. And it's easy to spot a psychotic when the disorder is characterized by fantasies. When there are no fantasies, it's difficult. Very difficult." He shook his head.

"When a young girl has a so-called 'nervous breakdown' in school, her fellow-pupils and instructors, her own father, are likely to shrug it off. There's no babbling of dreams and visions, no delusions of persecution, disorders of perception, no outward hysteria. The hysteria is all inside.

"When the young girl visits a psychoanalyst for treatment and develops a violent fixation on him, the world calls it love. They don't hear the panting confessions, the moans, the sobs, the threats of suicide.

"The analyst doesn't tell them, either, if he knows that the threats are genuine. If he feels that perhaps, in time, he can cure the disorder. Particularly, if he has the misfortune to fall in love with her. Actually it was pity; believe me in that, Dan, although I pity her no longer.

"You see, friends never know. They never see the violence, the manic rages, the frenzied, insensate clinging centered in the womb—the actual womb that brings hysteria to birth."

Ruppert gave me a half-grin and kept the other half for himself.

"It's funny, in a way, isn't it? A doctor married to a patient. And a patient besting the doctor. Because that's what happened. When she found out what was happening to herself, she couldn't stand the realization.

"Marriage, to Constance, symbolized an excuse for the abandonment of all repression. Our life together was not pleasant, I can assure you.

"As is characteristic in such cases, Constance began to project her guilt-fantasies onto me. *I* was the philanderer, the adulterer.

"I couldn't help her myself, and she repeatedly refused both analysis and consultation from others. I saw what was coming, but I could do nothing.

"There was a divorce—you must have heard about it by this time. Accusations, morbid, hysterical misinterpretations to the court."

"Why didn't you defend yourself?" I asked.

"Because I'm only an analyst part of the time, Dan. From the professional and ethical standpoint, perhaps I should have forced the issue—so that in the end Constance's condition would be recognized and proper treatment instituted.

"But besides being an analyst, I'm also a human being. A pretty weak one, too. And I couldn't take much more from that woman. I was willing to do almost anything, if only the relationship would end."

He rose. "I'm not asking you for sympathy, or making an explanation. I'm merely trying to give you a warning."

"You think I'm in danger?"

"Anyone who associates intimately with Constance is in danger," he told me. "As you know, I manage to keep a pretty close check on her activities. I feel that something will snap sooner or later—and when it does, I want to be on hand. To help her, to help anyone else who may be involved.

"That's the only way I can atone for my weakness in permitting her divorce to go through without revealing her actual condition. It's a debt I owe."

"But just what do you think she might do?"

"It's hard to say. You can't predict the actions of an alcoholic or a narcotic addict under excessive stimulation. And excessive sexual stimulation tends to operate in the same manner, in Constance's case. Acts of violence, infantile regression can be expected. Murder is one possibility . . . suicide, another.

"Whatever happens, I must do my best to stay on guard. And I wanted you to have the facts, and be prepared. You'd be doing a service to me, to Constance—to society, for that matter—if you felt free to report any symptoms which led you to suspect a crisis."

"Right."

I rose to go.

"One more thing, Dan. Be very careful. It may come without any prior indication, without warning. Keep your head."

We shook hands and I left.

So that's the way it is. You take the hard way up. You work like a dog. You do everything, risk putting your neck in a noose, just to get the breaks.

Then you get the breaks. Everything goes the way you planned and hoped.

Except that you can't have the one woman you want, and the woman you don't want may be screwy.

I walked uptown from Ruppert's office, thinking it over.

Everything added up to one sure thing—I had to get Constance Ruppert out of my life. Constance Ruppert, with her memory for faces, her dangerous capacity for hatred, and her still more dangerous capacity for love.

It was finished; I made up my mind to that. I wouldn't see her again. I'd take the risk of getting in bad with the Hollis firm—and it wasn't much of a risk, because the book was selling. Constance didn't like Jeff, but Hollis continued to issue printings of his book, because it sold.

But there was only one safe solution—I mustn't ever see Constance again.

By the time I got home, I was dead-tired. It hadn't been an easy day. First, Pat and the big letdown. Then Ruppert and his story. I gave up trying to figure out ways and means; what I wanted was twelve hours of sleep. No more thinking, no more worrying about Constance Ruppert.

I opened the door of the apartment and blinked. At first I thought I'd forgotten to turn out the light.

Then I saw her sitting there, and I understood. She smiled up at me expectantly, just as cool as if she were dressed.

"Hello, darling," said Constance.

XIV

The next morning I was pounding the typewriter in the front room when the doorbell rang.

It wasn't Constance, or Phil Teffner, or even a door-to-door salesman—though I'd gladly have settled for any of them, in preference to my visitor.

Lou King stood in the doorway.

"Well, this is a surprise! Come on in and make yourself at home, Lou. Why didn't you let me know you were coming to town?"

If he had, I could have managed to avoid him.

As King looked over the place, I hastily checked back to see if everything was all right. I had written to him when I hit town in

March, handing him a line as though I'd been in New York ever since quitting my job. Then he replied, telling me about Hazel Hurley's suicide. I answered him, deeply shocked and grieved to learn of her death.

It had all gone smoothly, as I'd expected. So why should I get nervous just because Lou King didn't say anything, just because he sat and looked at me, just because he didn't smoke, or smile, or even stir?

There was no reason for nervousness at all, but my hand shook when I tried to light a cigarette, and my voice broke as I asked, "How's every little thing with you, pal? Why haven't you written to me? What's the big idea?"

"Busy. What about you?"

"The same." I indicated the typewriter. "My royalty check won't come through for another six-seven months. Phil suggested I turn out a couple of slick shorts to tide me over and then get started on another novel. You seen Phil yet?"

"Had dinner with him yesterday. He's sold on you, Morley."

"Great guy. He's done a lot for me, and I owe you plenty for getting the two of us together. Teffner certainly helped in putting over the novel."

"The novel—it's going good, is it?"

"There'll be a third printing next month. Brings it up to nearly forty thousand."

"Well, it will have to sell a lot more than that before it's worth doing what you did to produce it."

"I don't get you."

"You get me, all right. What's the matter, Dan—do you think I don't know you killed Hazel Hurley?"

They say it's easier if you take it sitting down. I don't know. It didn't feel any easier to me.

After all, you sit down when they strap you into the chair, too. And Lou King was strapping me. He had on a blue suit, like a copper, and then a black robe, like a judge, and when I looked at his face I could see a warden and a priest, and the guy who pulls the switch.

But I sat there. What else could I do? I was afraid if I got up to run, I'd run the wrong way—toward Lou King, toward his throat.

I wanted to choke those words out of his throat, but I just sat there.

There were noises in my head: a hissing, like escaping gas, a roaring like an El train rounding the curve. Somehow his voice filtered through.

I opened my eyes and tried to stare him down, tried to listen. He kept right on talking.

"The whole business always sounded a little phony to me, Dan. I wondered about it at the time you quit your job. Then, the minute I read your book, everything fitted together perfectly. You killed Hazel Hurley—just as surely as if you actually murdered her."

"As if I *what*?"

"Oh, I know it isn't murder, legally speaking. But she wouldn't have committed suicide if you hadn't written that book about her."

All at once the lights came on again, and that tight feeling died away in my throat. I could even have smiled, but I didn't try to. I wanted to hear more, now.

"Everybody knew you ran out on Hazel, of course. She showed up a couple of times afterwards, ready to cry at the drop of a handkerchief, wanting to know if I'd heard from you—if anybody had heard from you. Didn't even have the decency to write to the girl, did you, Dan?

"That was a pretty lousy trick in itself; standing up a girl who was crazy about you, running away without any reason. I felt pretty ashamed for you even then.

"When she killed herself, people did a lot of talking—but I still wasn't sure. Couldn't figure it out. Then I read your book, and that told me everything I wanted to know."

King stood over me, twisting his hat in his hands.

"You drained that girl dry, didn't you, Morley? Drained her like some goddamned vampire—just to write a cheap book. Made her look like a tramp. Took all her confidences, all her secrets, and set them down on paper. Your heroine, Hedy, is Hazel all over.

"But that wasn't enough for you, was it? You had to go and show her the manuscript. That's what you did—told her just what you were writing and let her read it. Then you ran away, and left her to face the music.

"I don't know yet why you'd pull a dirty trick like that. I don't know why you hated her so, why you couldn't figure out what might happen. Maybe you knew what would happen, counted on it.

"Anyhow, you did it. And she killed herself. And I guess there's nothing anyone can do about it, and it's none of my business. But I couldn't hold up my own head until I got this chance to tell you what I think. For my dough, you're a cheap, double-crossing heel."

I started to get up, and he hit me in the mouth.

Off-balance, I fell back into the chair. By the time I got up again, he'd slammed the door behind him.

I rubbed my jaw. Lou King was a pretty flabby guy, and he couldn't hit very hard, but somehow it hurt like hell.

There wasn't a mark on my face when I took Constance to dinner that night. I looked like a million in a new blue flannel suit with a teal shirt and matching tie—much too good for the little night club we were sitting in. But the fall rain was coming down, and the place was just around the corner, and I needed a drink very badly.

A three-piece combo tried to slice the smoky air. A knife couldn't have done the job. Except for occasional bits of foot-work, you'd never have known that the crowd of drunks on the floor was supposed to be dancing. The management could have done better substituting a couple of trained chimps for their regular waiters; only I suppose it would have taken years to teach the chimps how to short-change customers with the same insolent dexterity.

But then, what do you want for twenty bucks—a good time, or something?

We sat there, drinking in the gay, cosmopolitan atmosphere, and a helluva lot of brandy.

I was beginning to get high, otherwise I'd have pulled out when the lights went out and the spot hit the dance floor.

Instead, I ordered another drink. The combo went into a fanfare, and something short and greasy padded out onto the floor. It wore a shoddy dress suit and a small child's felt hat. One hand manipulated a cigar while the other clutched the stand of a floor-mike.

It talked:

"Ha-ha, good evening everybody and welcome to the Comic Club. Well, we certainly have a great little crowd here tonight and I'm glad to see people of every sex in our audience and if that man in the purple tie is listening I'm only kidding, ha-ha. Well, we got a wonnerful show for all you lovely lovely people, and first of all I want to innerdooce a very outstanding artist and when you get a look at her from the front you'll unnerstan just what I mean, ha-ha."

"Dan, I want to talk to you."

"There's no voice I'd rather hear."

"Seriously, I mean."

"Here she is now and I want you kind folks to give her a big, big hand because, ha-ha, when you see her you'll agree she's the kind of a girl who can use a big big hand."

"I'm listening."

"Hand, I said, ha-ha."

"Phil Teffner introduced me to a friend of yours today."

"Really?"

"A man named Lou King. From Chicago."

"Here she is, the singing smiling star of our little show, the one, only, and inimitable Shirley Starr. All right everybody give for Shirley."

"King—oh, I remember him."

"He remembers you, too, Dan. He told me all about you when we had lunch together."

"You work fast, don't you?"

"So do you, according to King."

"Is that supposed to be a dirty crack? It's got a full set of earmarks."

"Don't be coy with me, Dan. Why haven't you ever told me about this girl—this Hazel Hurley?"

"Isn't a man entitled to a past?"

"Stop it, Dan. This is important to me. And I think it's going to be important to you, too."

"Deal the cards, Constance."

"You know what Lou King told me. About you and this girl. About how you wrote a book about her and left town, suddenly. About how she jumped in front of that El train."

"That's right. King thinks I'm a rat, doesn't he? And—just between the two of us—sometimes I think so, too. That's why I haven't told you, Connie. I'm trying to forget. That's why you're so good for me, darling. You help me to forget."

"Do I, darling?"

"You know you do."

"Then why don't we get married—right away?"

"Thank you, Shirley and thank you, ladies and gentlemen. Shirley will be back with us again in a little while, but now we gotta get on with the show. Great girl Shirley, ha-ha, you know there's only one thing wrong with her. In the first place she's too thin. And she's also too thin in the second place, ha-ha."

"You know what I told you, Connie. You've got too much money. It just wouldn't work. There's a name for guys who live off their wives."

"Don't be ridiculous, Dan!"

"I can't help the way I feel about such things. Give me a little time. I'm starting another book. If it goes, I should be able to count on a pretty decent income in the future. Then maybe we can work things out. In the meantime we're having a lot of fun, aren't we?"

"So the first queer says once a tomboy always a tomboy, ha-ha. All right, let it go, I got a million of 'em and they all stink."

"Is that what you told Hazel Hurley?"

"What do you mean?"

"King says you told Hazel you were going to marry her when your book was finished. King says Hazel was all broken up when you ran off and left her. King says——"

"King talks too much for his own good."

"You're right, Dan. You're so right! He talks entirely too much for his own good—and your own good, too."

"Now from the sublime to the ridiculuss I wanna have you all get acquainted with the next attraction in the Comic Club revue. Remember folks this is a revue not a floor show. We got a bunch of trained cockroaches for a floor show."

"What's all the mystery for, Constance?"

"There's no mystery. I'm just asking you to marry me."

"But——"

"Look, Dan. I know you don't love me. I know you don't want to marry me. I even know you can't bear to touch me unless you're crazy mad, or crazy drunk. Well, if that's the way it has to be, it's good enough for me. Because I want you, do you understand that? I want you, and I'm going to have you, and you'll get drunk if it's the only way, every single night for me——"

"Constance, what the hell——"

"You're going to be damned glad to marry me, darling. You're going to be damned glad that my money is on your side, and that I'll be on your side, keeping my mouth shut."

"This charming little hunk of femininity I said 'femininity' has studied three years in London, three years in Paris, and six years in vain. Here she is folks that interpetrer of terpchikory direct from the Styx Club in Hollywood, Miss Gracie La Grace."

"Jeff isn't the only one who knows a little psychology, my friend. You aren't going to stall me along the way you stalled Hazel Hurley, and then rig up a fake suicide——"

"What's that?"

"You can dispense with that, Dan. I always wondered why you were so uneasy every time I mentioned seeing you in Chicago.

And today, after talking to your friend King, I suddenly found out. I remember you quite clearly now—you and the color, red. Hazel Hurley had red hair, didn't she?"

"But——"

"And you didn't leave town. You must have hid out someplace, and Hazel Hurley found you. So you took her out and got her drunk—I saw you that night at a place on Wabash, I know that definitely—and then you pushed her in front of the El."

"That was wonnerful Gracie and I know all the folks here want to see more of you but there's a law ha-ha."

"Your imagination's working overtime, Connie."

"Well, yours had better stop working—because it won't do any good. No, I didn't say anything to King. But after I left him, I managed to ask Phil Teffner just when you showed up in New York. And that checked, too. Because you quit your job in Chicago in February to leave town, according to King. And Phil Teffner knows you didn't arrive in New York until March 14. Hazel Hurley died in Chicago on the twelfth."

"You're crazy."

"That's right. Crazy with happiness. Because we're going to get married, Dan. Right away. We'll find a house and buy furniture and settle down, and you'll never hear anything from me about this whole business again. If you behave."

The chill rain was still falling as we hit the street. Constance shivered and came close to me. I shivered, too.

"It's getting cold, darling," she said.

"I know."

"From now on I'm taking an interest in your health. You ought to dress more warmly."

"All right."

"You know, you really ought to start wearing a scarf."

"Yeah," I said. "Maybe I should."

XV

I never did find out whether or not it's pleasant to be the author of a fast-selling novel. Between Constance and the black notebook, I didn't get much spare time.

I didn't take it lying down. I sweated over some slick, short stuff, but it didn't work out, and I couldn't seem to get started on my novel, either. The plot for *Lucky Lady* was all outlined and Teffner had given it his okay, but the writing came hard. In fact, it didn't come at all.

Constance was in the book, of course. A scheming, sexed-up bitch who killed one man to marry another, only to be murdered herself. The murder device was very simple—somebody poured oil in her bathtub so she'd slip while drunk. Really nothing to it, I could think of a hundred ways to kill a woman like Constance.

As a matter of fact, I did think of hundreds of ways. I dreamed about killing her every night.

So I was really in no shape to write, even though Teffner screamed at me to get going, capitalize on the reception of the first book.

Constance wanted me to write, too.

"Don't you worry about anything else," she told me. "I'm going to find us a house at once—leave all that to me."

She was serious, deadly serious. Deadly is a word I often thought of in connection with Constance. But I dared not do anything; better to kill her off in the story.

I'll always remember those late fall afternoons when we went house-hunting in the second-hand coupé I'd picked up.

"Why don't we wait?" I kept asking. "You know what the housing situation is. We'll never find a place."

"I'll get one, wait and see."

Sometimes I got dizzy spells and pulled up on the side of the road for a few minutes.

"Poor boy, you're wearing yourself out. You should be home, writing. Let me handle this."

"You really love me, don't you, Constance?"

"Yes, I do. And you really hate me."

"How can you say that?"

"It's true. You hate me, and I hate myself for wanting you. You can't understand that, can you?" And those full lips would press down on mine, mushrooming, opening with a life of their own. The lips saying the words meant one thing. The lips seeking mine meant another. I'd stand it as long as I could and then pull away. And the lips would speak again.

"Do you think it's any fun for me, being in love with a murderer?"

"But that's nonsense, Connie. I've explained——"

"Oh, never mind. You're marrying me to cover up, and we both know it. And I'm marrying you because I have to have you. You don't know what's wrong with me, do you, Dan? You don't know how I feel. I realize just what you are, and what I am, but when I'm with you, I feel. . . ."

Then she'd tell me how she felt, in detail. And show me. It wasn't nice. Jeff Ruppert was right about her. She wasn't sane.

But I would marry her. I knew that.

And so the headaches got worse, and the writing didn't jell, and at night she'd come to my place and there was nothing to do but drink and try to hold back.

She was thin, and she had a double chin, and the skin on her neck was leathery. The worst part of it was when her eyes bulged and she kept whimpering in a high voice like a hurt kitten, only she wanted to be hurt——

I began to dream about killing her when I wasn't asleep.

Finally, I took refuge in bodily illness in order to escape. Psychosomatic fugue.

According to Dr. Endicott, I had flu.

Anyhow, I was propped up in bed that Sunday when Pat and Jeff paid me a call.

"Don't bother to play host," Pat said. "We just dropped in for a minute to see how you were."

"It's nothing," I croaked. "Just a touch. Too much running around in the rain."

"I hear you found a place," Jeff remarked.

"Not exactly. You know, Constance has been looking for weeks—but I finally got hold of a real estate man Friday with a house out Asbury Park way. We were supposed to have a look at it today, but you see how things are."

"Tough."

"When are you two getting married?" I asked.

Pat blushed. "Not for a while yet. You know I'm going out to the Coast to handle Phil's office there. And Jeff is trying to arrange things so he can join me. Maybe we'll be settled by spring."

"You and Constance will be an old married couple by then," Ruppert said.

I avoided looking at him.

The door clicked in the front room, and Connie came in. Nobody seemed in the least embarrassed because she had her own key to my place. I covered up my own feelings with a coughing spell.

"Poor darling!" She bundled the covers up around my neck. "And here I thought we were all set to look at the house. I don't suppose you'd dare go in this downpour."

I shook my head, still coughing. "Not a chance. Doc Endicott promised to look in here about four."

Connie grinned, a trifle maliciously, I thought, at Pat and Jeff.

"I promise you he won't get sick when I take care of him," she announced. "But Dan—what about Mr. Miller? Do you think he might take me out to see the place?"

"I thought of that myself, and I've been trying to call him all morning. No answer."

"Damn. Then we'll lose it."

"Why? After all, you've got the key."

"So I have."

"And Miller knows we planned to inspect it. Tell you what, why don't you just take a drive out to Asbury Park and see how it looks to you? I trust your judgment. Then you can stop in here on your way back and let me know. Maybe Pat and Jeff would drive along."

"Sorry," said Ruppert. "We have a date. Got to be getting along. But it sounds like a sensible idea to me, Constance."

"Good enough." Connie fumbled in her purse. "Here's the address. Now don't tell me I forgot the key!"

I shook my head. "You didn't. Like a sensible girl, you left it with me for safekeeping Friday night. And here it is."

I took it from the bureau top beside the bed.

"Hand me my sulfa tablets on the way out," I called. "Endicott is going to be mighty upset if my fever isn't down when he gets here."

Jeff grinned at me. "Too bad you didn't call me in on this case. I'd gladly have taken care of you for nothing."

"Yeah," I said. "That's what I was afraid of."

It was a good enough exit line for all of them. They trooped out, chattering, and I sat there staring at the rain beyond the window.

I sat there staring at the rain beyond the window. It was quite dark, and the shadows whispered. Of course they weren't really whispering, it was just the fever. Fever, whispering in my head.

Then there was another noise. Footsteps, from far away. Footsteps echoing downstairs, echoing in emptiness. Footsteps on the stairs, in the hall. Slow, uncertain footsteps. The cautious tread of a stranger in a strange place. A dark place. Footsteps in my skull.

The footsteps were halting outside the door now. I saw the knob turning, a million miles away. Turning—the dull globe of a revolving world.

She came in.

"Oh! What are you doing here?"

"Waiting. For you."

"But how did you get in?"

"Skeleton key."

Skeleton key. Skeletons in the closet. I could hear them rattling. They mustn't rattle. Turn the key and make them stop. Echoes and footsteps rattling in my head.

"I don't understand—you were home, in bed. You're sick, Dan."

"I know. But I had to come. I wasn't sure I could beat you here, but I tried. You always drive slowly in the rain, don't you, Constance? I drive fast. And I made it."

"For a surprise?"

"Of course. You didn't think I'd really let you come here all alone, did you? To such a big, dark, deserted house." I looked around the upstairs bedroom, leaning back against the window-sill, steadying myself. "Well, what do you think of the place?"

She came close, quite close.

"I don't like it, Dan. It's just frame, to begin with. And it smells funny; like oil, or something."

"That's from the burner in the basement, I suppose. I went down and fiddled around. Cold in here."

She was very close to me.

"Dan, what's the matter with you?"

"Nothing."

"But you look so—oh, you shouldn't have done this, darling. You're really quite ill, you know."

"I know. The important thing is, I'm not too sick."

"Not too sick?"

Then I had the scarf out, my hands up and over her throat.

I knew it was all right, I wasn't too sick, and I could hold her even though she struggled. I held her very tightly because I wanted her to hear every word.

"Yes, I'm not too sick to kill you. And I'm going to kill you, because I can't stand the sight of you. Because I won't marry you, and you know all about Chicago. I did murder Hazel and I'm going to murder you."

The scarf held her, but she could still manage to gasp.

"Dan, you can't! Please—I'll forget everything, I swear it! I won't tell, you know I won't. I'll go away. You don't have to do this—you can trust me—I promise!"

Her voice gurgled like water in a faucet. I turned it off. But she could still hear me, hear me as I whispered, "But you don't understand, Connie. Keeping still about things won't help you a bit. Because I want to kill you. Do you know that? I want to kill you. I'm enjoying it, this is what I've waited for—what I've dreamed!"

I'd seen her eyes bulge before, heard her whimper; but never like this. And then the folds of the maroon scarf lapped over her face as I wound it tighter and tighter.

XVI

Doc Endicott didn't get over to my place until after five, and by that time I was safely back in bed. And I really was running a high fever.

He looked in again the next morning, but I can't say I remember anything about his visit. I knew he thought it was pneumonia, and he tried to get me into a hospital but couldn't.

He must have sent the nurse over instead, because the next thing I remember, she was sitting there and I was yelling for water. Only I wasn't really yelling, just whispering.

It was pretty bad, at that. By the time the fever went down Thursday afternoon I was a wreck. Friday was almost gone before they let me have any visitors.

Teffner was the boy who broke the news.

I'd paved the way, of course—as much as anybody can pave the way with a temperature of 104° to cramp his style. But even during the worst part of it, I remembered one thing; I had to keep hold of myself, keep my mouth shut. And I had to remember to call for Constance, occasionally.

From Wednesday on, I asked for her continually. They must have told Teffner that before he came in.

"Endicott says you had a pretty narrow squeak," he began.

"I guess so," I whispered, feeling sorry for him already.

"But you're coming along all right now—well enough to take a shock."

"Shock?"

He leaned over me. Without anyone to put a cigarette in his mouth he looked pretty shaky. I felt sorrier than ever for him. But I had to play this thing out all the way.

"It's about Constance."

"Yes—where is she? Why hasn't she come to see me?"

"She won't be coming."

"What are you talking about?"

"Dan—Connie's dead."

But why drag it out? I made the usual noises, listening very carefully for the explanations.

It seems Constance had left my place early Sunday afternoon with Jeff and Pat. She had driven out alone to this house to make an inspection. Apparently she found the place a little too chilly when she arrived and decided to turn on the oil heater in the basement before looking around. The heater must have been defective—there was an explosion. Whether it killed her outright or merely stunned her the investigators couldn't determine. In any event the frame house, despite the rain, burned very quickly. By the time an alarm was given by a passing motorist it was too late. When the engines arrived the entire structure was in flames. The basement and first floor were completely destroyed. Connie's car was found parked in the driveway. Actual identification of her body was made, but it proved to be no easy task under the circumstances.

The news had been kept from me, even though the funeral services had already been conducted. I might have been questioned, except that Ruppert and Pat and Dr. Endicott had all been on hand to testify for me at the inquest. My incapacity was self-evident, and apparently the investigators were satisfied with the findings.

Teffner knew how I must feel about the tragedy, and there was nothing he could say to help me at a time like this.

That's what *he* thought. Actually, his words were the best medicine in the world. After he left, I could lie back and take it easy. I could go over it all again in my mind: dragging the body downstairs, setting the burner and spreading the oil; waiting for the fire to start and catch hold, and then making that mad dash home in the car. I had been pretty woozy during the last stages, barely remembering to get rid of the skeleton key—and I wondered if I had slipped up on any of the details.

Apparently I hadn't.

And then, again——

Then again, there was Jeff Ruppert. He didn't show up until the following Tuesday. By that time I was sitting in the front room and the nurse had left. I was shaved, dressed, and felt at least 70 per cent out of a possible 100.

At least I did until Jeff arrived.

"Feeling better?"

"Physically, yes."

"Feel well enough to talk about it yet?"

"Rather not."

"I see."

"But I do want to thank you and Pat for testifying for me at the inquest."

"Yes. And that's what I wanted to discuss. You know, after I left you that afternoon, I got to worrying a bit. You didn't look too good."

"I didn't feel too good. Endicott can tell you that."

"He has."

I turned, quickly, but Ruppert was doing the inevitable with his pipe and I couldn't see his face.

"Anyway, Dan, I called you around four o'clock. That is, I tried to call you. But there was no answer."

"Oh—it was you who called! Seems to me I remember a phone ringing somewhere and it bothered me. I guess I just plain passed out."

"But you let Dr. Endicott in at 5:10."

"Sure I did. I felt a little stronger then—say, just what is this?"

"Take it easy, Dan. Only conversation."

"But I don't like to talk about it."

"All right. Just one thing more, before I forget—was your coupé in the garage all day Sunday?"

"Sure. That is, I guess so. Unless Connie drove it out to—to that place. She has—had—the keys. Why? Isn't it in the garage now?"

"It is. But the garage man—oh, skip it, Dan. He just thought you might have taken the car out—but he was very busy and couldn't be sure. I guess I'm as emotionally upset about this as you are."

Emotionally upset. Not nervous, not jittery. Emotionally upset—a psychoanalyst's term. That was the clue. The only clue to getting out of this, distracting him. I had to risk it.

"Listen, Jeff."

"I'm listening."

"I've changed my mind. I want to talk about it. It's getting so I have to talk about it. And I might as well tell you—no one has a better right to know."

He wasn't fiddling with his pipe now; he was all business. I imagine he wished he had a stenotypist ready to take it down.

I put my head down between my hands and began to mumble very slowly, gradually increasing the pitch and tempo of my voice.

"Maybe I'm going nuts. I don't know. That's why I'm talking to you—you'd be able to see the picture. But ever since Constance left that Sunday—all through the fever, the delirium, everything—I've had a funny hunch something was wrong. Even before Teffner told me what happened, it was as if I knew. I kept calling for Connie—calling for her. . . ."

"Yes. The nurse told me."

So the little rat had checked on that, too!

"Because you see, Jeff, I wasn't going to marry Connie."

That was a dangerous thing to say. Everything I told him would be dangerous, but there was a chance he'd heard it already, from Constance. Better to take the risk of letting him hear it from me than try to conceal it and let him make his own deductions. So I went on, building it up.

"No, Jeff. I couldn't marry her. You told me so, yourself. You warned me, remember?"

"That's right. And you told her so?"

"Not in as many words. But she was beginning to realize a break was coming. And a couple of nights before she staged a very melodramatic scene—complete with threats of suicide. Of course, that didn't impress me too much at the time. Why, you spoke to me several times about that; saying she might have suicidal impulses."

"True. But just what are you trying to say?"

"Jeff, it may sound screwy as hell, but I have a feeling Connie wasn't killed accidentally. It might have been suicide."

"But the coroner and the insurance investigators. . . ."

"They could be wrong, couldn't they? Look: you and I know Connie better than they ever could. Think of the situation. That's all I can think of, it preys on me night and day—Connie coming up here, knowing we're going to split up. Meeting you and Pat, both happy. Putting on a gay pose in front of her ex-husband and his new sweetheart and going out to look at a house she'll never live in. Going into that house, that cold, chill house; it must have been dark and empty in the rain. Standing there and thinking it over in the silence, wondering if——"

"You tell it as if you'd actually seen the place."

"I do see it!" I let my voice come up full. "I see it in my dreams! She killed herself. Just like——"

Then I caught it, broke it off. He tensed.

"Just like—who?"

"Like—Hazel. You didn't know about Hazel, did you, Jeff? She was a Chicago girl. She and I were engaged out there. Well, we had a quarrel. I left town when I completed my book and came here. And about a month afterward she—killed herself."

"Over you?"

"Of course. What other reason could she have? Oh, you needn't take my word for it. Ask Teffner's friend, Lou King. I used to work for him. He knows. He as much as told me it was my leaving Hazel that caused her to commit suicide. I'm guilty, Jeff, guilty as if I'd murdered her. And now, perhaps I've murdered Connie too."

"Take it easy, Dan. You're not completely well yet. You're not thinking clearly."

"I don't have to think. I *know*! But why is it, Jeff? What's wrong with me, why do I cause such things? What can I do? For God's sake, help me!"

I don't remember exactly what he said. Everything was anticlimax from that point on. He comforted me. He reassured me. He went to work and pointed out that it was manifestly impossible for either Hazel Hurley or Constance Ruppert to have died in any way except by accident. He cited cases and precedent. And I sat there, fully realizing the benefits of the psychoanalytical approach.

If I had kept a diary of daily events, the next five months would be virtually blank.

I got well. I kept out of bars, away from parties and people. I wrote *Lucky Lady*. I revised a portion of it. Hollis accepted the manuscript. Somewhere around that time Pat and Ruppert both left for the Coast. She went in January and he in March. Our farewells were casual. I saw to that. The whole episode was closed, and it must remain closed.

That's all.

Except for the dreams. While I was writing, going at it eight, ten hours a day, I didn't have any dreams.

It was only toward the last, when the revisions were being completed, that the nightmares came.

I don't know what I might have done about them, because right in the middle of nothing came the big explosion.

Teffner, on the telephone, saying, "How fast can you get down to the office, Dan?"

"What's up?"

"Nothing much. Only Sam Hague just bought your book from galley proofs."

"Sam Hague? Who the hell is he?"

"Nobody at all but one of the biggest independent producers in the game."

"Movies, you mean?"

"I've got a check for fifty thousand down here waiting for you that has movies written all over it."

"I'm on my way."

"Better pack your bag, son. Because I think I'm also selling you along with the book. I can get you at least a three-month deal on the strength of it, if you're ready to take it."

"Phil, do you know something?"

"What?"

"I love you."

I hung up. My hand trembled so that I could scarcely get the receiver back in its cradle.

This was it, I kept telling myself in the car going down. This was it, the real top, two books and royalty checks and movie money and a job with a studio, and nobody knew and nobody would ever know because I'd pulled it off, I was safe, this was the big time, so sing it and sing it loud, California here I come.

But I didn't really sing until the thought suddenly hit me. Pat Collins was out there.

The Black Notebook

Maybe I'm taking it too seriously. I don't know. Perhaps I should have been born in another time. A few hundred years ago there wouldn't have been any doubts about the importance of murder.

There was a day when the sanctity of life was all-important; a time when life was a sacrament. If you took a life you damned your immortal soul. Everybody knew that.

In those days, murder had a real meaning. To you. To God, and the Devil.

Take Gilles de Rais, for example. He knew what he was doing. He was an instrument of Satan. And for all we know, Jack the Ripper might have considered himself an instrument of God.

There's something to think about. I often wonder what went on in their minds—Doctor Crippen, Cream, Landru, and all the rest.

I've been reading up on them all, lately. It's only natural that I should.

Why not? Doesn't a novice priest read the Bible?

I've often felt that if I could only understand *them*, I'd know a little more about my own problem.

Consider Springheel Jack.

Most people probably have never heard of him. Murder isn't important any more, is it? Springheel Jack is only a name, and for all anyone knows, I made it up.

Only I didn't. There was a Springheel Jack, and the people who were his contemporaries in London in 1838 had a little more respect for murder. Because Springheel Jack was abroad——

In the dark, twisted streets and tangled alleys of London's night-town, crouching behind trees and hedges, something lurked.

It may have been a man. It may have been a demon.

They called it "Springheel Jack" because it appeared and disappeared so quickly.

It walked upon two legs—that much is known. It wore a long black cloak when it rose out of hiding to confront a victim; but not for long.

Almost immediately the cloak would be cast aside, revealing that which lay beneath—a manlike body that glowed in the dark. The body glowed, and the face glowed, and the eyes blazed, while the mouth opened to shoot out tongues of blue and white flame.

Victims fainted at the sight—fainted and died beneath rending claws.

One set of claws was found later; hollow structures of brass moulded to fit over hands and fasten to wrists by means of leather straps. (Whose hands? Whose wrists?)

Several of the intended victims escaped and lived to tell the tale, but it was always the same tale—the cloaked, silent figure rising out of the night and the fog; the blazing body and fiery eyes; the mouth that breathed living flame.

Through the winter and into the spring it prowled unchecked—only to disappear forever as summer came.

He was a madman. He was a chemist. He was not he, but *it*—a demon. Everybody had a theory. But no one knew. No one ever knew.

Springheel Jack came, killed, and vanished; just as Jack the Ripper did fifty years later; just as half a dozen maniacs, monsters, murderers did and always will be doing.

Why?

I'd like to think there was a reason behind it all. That there always have been and always will be a few men in the world who dare to dramatize death—give it a meaning.

Men who dare to say, "Too bad there isn't an actual Grim Reaper, swinging the sharp scythe to slay. Too bad there is no Satan, walking the world for souls to snare.

"I'll remedy the deficiency. I'll be Satan, I'll be Death. Look into my bony skull sockets and see if you can read the secrets of the eyes that are not there. Read my riddle—why does a death's-head always grin?"

Come to think of it—why *does* a skull grin? Maybe Spring-heel Jack knew. Maybe Landru, de Rais, the Ripper knew.

Maybe, some day, I'll know, too.

No, it's no use. I'm never going to figure it out. I know that now. I was going to write down just how I felt. Analyze everything, bit by bit, and try to understand.

Well, I've done my best. I've tried to pluck the little black butterflies out of my brain and pin them down under the microscope—tried to point out why they resembled death's-head moths.

But I've failed.

I still don't know what made me kill Rena, what made me kill Hazel.

Looking back, it doesn't make sense to me. If I was disgusted with Rena and wanted her money, why didn't I just steal the dough and then blow town, fast? I could have gotten into her place any time I wanted to. Maybe she'd even have given me the money if I asked her. There were a dozen other ways of getting it from her. So why did I kill her?

And Hazel. She never harmed me. She loved me, she did everything she could, gave everything she was capable of giving. If I didn't want to marry her, why couldn't I figure an easier out? An abortion, something like that. At the worst, I might have run away and attempted to hide if I was afraid to face the music. Why did I kill her? Why was that the first thought in my head, even when I got drunk?

What's gone wrong with me? Calling myself crazy won't solve anything. A label isn't an explanation. Besides, lots of people blow their tops every day, and most of them never have any urge to murder. If it is an urge.

Questions, endless questions, and never an answer. No answers at all.

Why must I write about it? Why put it all on paper, where somebody might run across it? Why take the risk?

What good does it do to torment myself, what kind of a compulsion drives me?

It's no good. I can't tell anything more. I can't tell how I really feel and why. I can't tell what makes me different from anyone else.

I walk and talk and eat and sleep. I ride the same train as my neighbors, read the same newspaper, smoke the same brand of cigarettes. I've said that before, but it continues to fascinate me. The idea of being the same, yet different inside.

Nobody knows about it. My neighbors don't recognize me for what I am. They couldn't possibly. I can pitch a fast line of chatter. I'm a sharp dresser. I know my way around.

I've fooled them all in my time. Tough precinct captains, plainclothes men, jungle 'bos. I made my living the hard way for years. Nobody tumbled.

Look how I pulled the wool over Rena's eyes, and King's, and Teffner's, and Hazel's, and all the rest of them. Even Ruppert couldn't figure it all out.

I'm one guy who can say he's gotten away with murder—and *prove* it.

Calling myself crazy won't answer it. Nobody bothers to count my buttons for me. They all think I'm O.K. And a lot smarter than most other guys, for that matter.

Sure. That must be it. I'm smarter. I know more angles and I play more angles. So why in hell do I bother with any explanations, even to myself?

The only difference between myself and the rest is that I'm smarter. I know how to get what I want and get away with it.

There. I found out for myself, after all. And it's a good thing, because it was beginning to get on my nerves—all this stuff about dreams and theories and half-baked memories.

Now I won't have to write about it any more. I don't need to keep notes. It's going to be a lot easier that way. And a lot safer.

I won't need my notebook, I won't have to come running to my little black crutch for support.

What a fool I was! Sitting around and scribbling in it like

some half-baked schoolgirl writing down her daydreams in a Secret Diary.

I'm beyond all that. There's nothing to worry about, nothing to think about. I can go my own way. There is no Rena any more, no Hazel, no Constance.

Rena is only a bundle of rotting bones in an unmarked grave. The flame is extinguished in the clotted curls that cling to Hazel's skull. And Constance is enjoying a final ravishment by a long white worm——

Stop that! I said I'd stop, and I will stop. They're dead and buried, all of them. Now I must bury the memories.

Yes, there's only one thing wrong with me—I insist on stirring it all up again with this notebook.

Keeping the notebook, that's what makes me different.

That's the answer.

And from now on, I won't keep it any more. From now on, everything is going to be all right.

HOLLYWOOD

XVII

"So YOU wanna know all about Hollywood?" said the bald-headed man. He was very drunk, and he had trouble raising his glass from the table as the train lurched through the night. The club car was deserted, and I couldn't escape him even if I tried. Not that I did try. Anything was better than going back to that compartment, trying to sleep.

"First trip out, eh, Morley?" he grunted, deep in his glass. "God, I remember mine. Back in '24. I worked for FBO that stretch. Good old FBO! Don't suppose you even know the name. Before your time."

"Right," I said. "Sam, another of the same for myself and Mr.——"

"Ainsworth. Lloyd Ainsworth! That's a laugh, son. Was a time the name meant something."

I stared at him. All the name meant to me was a drunken, bald-headed old coot in a suit two sizes larger than necessary. Maybe the suit had fitted him, once. Maybe the liquor had shriveled him up. I didn't know, didn't care. He was somebody to talk to, or at least listen to. Right now I had no chance to do more than listen.

"Serials were big stuff in those days," he said. "We shot 'em off the cuff. Remember *The Million Dollar Mystery? The Adventures of Maisie?* There was one gag in there, when Al Cooke and Kit Guard tried to climb down the fire escape with snowshoes on—ah, to hell with it! You aren't interested, are you?"

"On the contrary," I murmured, twirling my swizzle stick.

"Don't be polite," said Ainsworth. "I know what it is when they get polite. The old finger. I get it all the time now, the finger. Did Jimmie Cruze ever give me the finger? Or Tom Ince? Murnau paid me fifteen hundred a week! That was top money in those days, son. I did a screenplay once for Charley Ray. Ready to sink my own dough into it when he went bust. First time I got the finger was after that, from Cosmopolitan."

He scowled. "Know what I'm doing now? Westerns! Goddam quickie, on-the-cuff westerns. Why, I didn't even handle that stuff when I went with FBO—never wrote a line for anybody less than Jack Mulhall or Lew Cody. He's dead now."

Ainsworth gulped his drink. Sam, at the bar, was ready. The bottle descended and an amber arc shot into the glass, slopped over the side. The bald-headed man's eyes blinked with the effort of following the movement.

"Hell, they're all dead now. Sometimes I think I'm living in a goddam graveyard. Milton Sills and House Peters, Lloyd Hamilton—you don't remember Lloyd, do you? There was a comic for you! Burned out. Snitz Edwards, and Karl Dane. Dane and Arthur. And Langdon. Keaton's still around, though. But old Mack Swain is gone; remind me to tell you the time I almost worked for Chaplin, it's a riot. Did you see Syd Chaplin in The *Better 'Ole?*"

He was talking drunk, now. I couldn't follow him. "Priscilla Dean," he muttered. "Wheeler Oakman." It was a catalogue, free fantasy. Free, except that I paid for the drinks.

"Dead, so many dead. Dressier and Tashman and Flora Finch, Tellegen and good old Tommie Meighan. He used to work out at Astoria. About the time Harry Myers made the first *Connecticut Yankee.* I scripted one for Lupino Lane once, but he never went over here. Like Max Davidson. Both dead, now. So is Wolheim and Ben Turpin and Georgie Beban. And Louis Mann, that temperamental—oh, what do you care? What does anybody care? You don't even know the names, do you? They were all up there, once. Norman Kerry, Barbara La Marr—what a honey she was!—Marguerite de la Motte, she used to work with Fairbanks—Ray McKee and Ray Griffiths, too! Ernest Torrence was a pal of mine. He and Dick Talmadge. Dead. I oughta lay down and die, myself. One more finger and I'll be ready."

The red eyes sought mine.

"Watch out for that finger, son. You may think I'm playing the heavy, but you'll learn. I could give you a hundred names that were top b.o. just twenty years ago—hell, fifteen!—and you wouldn't remember one of them. Stars, the biggest, and still alive. But they got the finger. Just like the ones I did name, the dead ones. They got the finger, too. Death goosed them. Believe me, they were the lucky ones—they didn't have to stick around and take it every day. The way I'm taking it. The way you'll take it if you're not careful."

"Thanks," I said. "I'll watch my step."

"I'm not talking about watching your step," Ainsworth said. "That won't help. I'm talking about getting out when you've had enough. Getting out while you're still up there, while you can. Because there's nothing to watch. Nothing to learn."

"Don't kid me. Every racket has its angles. You must know plenty of them."

"The only angle is that there isn't any angle." Ainsworth reached for my drink and downed it. "That's why nobody has ever written a really good book about Hollywood. West, Shulberg, McCoy, Pollack, even old Scott Fitzgerald took a crack at it. They each got some of it down on paper, but there's so much you can't capture. So much."

The whistle cut through his words. I began to nod. Maybe I could sleep after all, get away from this old bore and really sleep——

"Don't go yet. Lemme tell you what I mean. About no angles. No answers. Why is it that every picture with the word 'dark' in the title makes money? I'm asking you a fair question, isn't it so? Just answer that one. Every picture with the word 'dark' in the title makes dough. So what's the reason? Nobody knows.

"Last decent break I got, it was on a mystery. Full credit assignment, so I won't mention names. We ran it through before cutting and just after the chase the producer yells, 'Give me lights!' I ask politely what the hell's the big idea, there's five minutes to go and all the explanation coming yet. 'The dog runs sixty-eight minutes as is,' he says. 'That's long enough for a B thriller.' I just stare at him. After twenny years in the racket I can only stare. 'But what about the explanation?' So he tells me, 'We don't need any explanation. The audience doesn't want one. It drags the whole picture. Cut it out and run as is.' So the lousy dog grosses over eight hundred grand, good money for any B, and what's the answer? A mystery without explanations! That's the Industry for you."

I shook my head.

"Then why are you going back?"

"For the finger." Ainsworth smiled. He was beginning to drool a little, and the smile was not pleasant. "Why kid myself? I know I got it coming and I'm gonna get it. One way or the other, it's the finger for everybody who stays in too long. Maybe the fat one, from some producer. Maybe that bony one I was talking about, from old man Death. But after a while, you stick in this game and you get like a picture yourself. You keep running until they holler, 'Cut!' on you. The old finger."

I edged out of the car and swayed back to my compartment. There would be no dreams, no nightmares tonight. That's because I wouldn't sleep. I'd be lying there awake, trying to figure it all out. Wondering if twenty years from now I'd be riding a train and mumbling in my beard to some young punk about the good old days.

Get out while the getting is good. While you're on top. Don't wait for the finger. We all get the finger sooner or later. How soon would it happen to me? Maybe he was right. More right than he dreamed. Maybe the time to get out was now, before anything could happen. Why should I risk it? What chance did I have of lasting a year, let alone twenty years? Where would I end up?

To hell with it. The important thing was, I knew where I'd be tomorrow.

Hollywood.

XVIII

You can label almost anybody by finding out what time they go to work in the morning.

The six-o'clock people are the scum of the earth, and they know it. They sit stiffly, crowded together in streetcars and busses like an immobile cargo of corpses. Sleep is sour in their mouths.

They hate their jobs, they hate each other, they hate themselves. But they're too tired to care.

At seven, the stupor has vanished from commuting faces, to be replaced by snarling scowls. The seven-o'clock people hate everything too, but they have the energy to express it. They move briskly; they push, shove, elbow, grumble, curse. They dress a little better than the janitors and elevator operators who warmed the seats they now occupy. Some of them earn good money in factories, sweatshops, service-trades; but they earn it the hard way.

Eight o'clock is the hour of the timid soul. The newspaper reader, the rental book girls who work in the big offices where the manager checks on how long they stay in the washroom. The clerks, the business school graduates, the students; the white-shirt-and-conservative-tie men and the tailored-suit-and-red-nail polish girls. They behave quite decorously. Somebody might be waiting, watching, noticing, singling them out for that big break. They are self-conscious. Who knows? The man sitting across the aisle might be Mr. Big himself, Mr. Future Husband, Mr. Better Boss, Mr. John W. God.

The nine o'clockers are positively gay. Business and professional men, assistant managers, competent girls who really run the whole office, people whose cars are laid up, who left the car at home for the wife today. They have friends; they talk volubly and make dates for lunch. Men get up and give their seats to women; men sit down and stare at legs.

The ten o'clock crowd—oh, but you never see them, and they're not a crowd. Just a bunch of single drivers, bowling along in big cars with the radio going full blast, taking the longer route because it's more pleasant, reaching over to pat the fat pigskin briefcase, reaching into pockets to fumble with the monogrammed presentation wallet stuffed with checkbooks and plane tickets and membership cards. They're the elite, the cream accounts for salesmen and credit agencies and banks—the good risks, the good providers, the good fellows.

Of course, every crowd has its share of phonies. One of the six A.M. boys has a pair of loaded dice in his pocket and one of the ten A.M. executives carries a prospectus for watered stock. But the type remains constant, the breed is true.

That's how I always rated people, and I thought I knew them all.

Then I went to Hollywood and met the ultimate—the guy who doesn't go to work at any hour. He stays home and you come to him.

We were sitting on the flat-topped sundeck of the big pink stucco house overlooking the beach.

A big Scott over in the corner blared out at full volume, and he talked against it, talked over it. No liquor or cigars for him—he didn't believe in stimulants, just an endless dosage of sound, something to fight against.

He looked like a fighter, sitting there hunched over in a bathrobe, hairless sunbaked skull resting on his shoulders like an orange balanced on a piano crate.

Sentences strained through the *Scythian Suite.*

"We're going to get along, Morley. I like what you say—you don't know anything about pictures. You got the honest attitude. So don't worry.

"Hague doesn't make mistakes. I didn't bring you out because I thought you could write for pictures. I didn't buy your story because it was a good yarn, either."

His thumb—a weenie encircled by a diamond ring—prodded my knee.

"Nothing personal, Morley. Hague's talking pictures now. Your book—it has no basic story line. But it's a vehicle!

"Get it? Hague's an indie. Release tie-ups, but no studio. I buy my writers, my production staff, my stars. When Hague gets a chance to sign up a big name for a one-pic deal, Hague signs. Even if there's no story for the name. For my money, to hell with a story—give me a vehicle for a star. That's your *Lucky Lady.* A vehicle."

Prokofieff's finale gave way to the introduction to *Song of the Nightingale.* Hague's voice was up to it.

"So don't you worry about a thing, Morley. I'm not asking you to even do a treatment. This I can buy. But I want you to stick around, read the treatment, stay with it until we get a shooting script. Give it your slant. Make suggestions. Build up that lead, what's-her-name. All you got to do is keep in touch. I'll put a couple a men on it and in a week we'll be ready to talk production. I'd like to use somebody like Stanwyck, if the schedule works out."

So far, what with Sam Hague and the Russians making all the noise, I hadn't said much of anything.

"But don't I have a place to work?" I asked.

"Stay home. Go out, enjoy yourself. I don't care. Just so you hop right over here when I call you. We'll work here, talk things out. A regular Sam Hague Production."

He sat back. A record side ended, and unaccountably, the machine began to play an old Fats Waller number.

"You'll catch on, Morley. Why, you're beginning to look like a regular Hollywood type already, with that scarf you're wearing."

By good luck I'd lined up a little bungalow out in Beverly Hills, on the wrong side of Wilshire. It turned out to be only a short walk to Teffner's coast office, over near the bank.

In the outer office, the kind of a girl who wears Harlequin frames told me to go right in.

I went right in.

Pat was wearing her hair in an upsweep and she had her special perfume all over her neck.

"Dan! I've been expecting you."

Her hands were cool. She had blunt, babyish thumbs.

"Tell me all about it—did you see Hague yet?"

I told her all about it.

"You're a bright boy, Dan. Sam Hague is a hard one to handle. He knows what he wants, and he gets it. Just keep it up—let him do all the arranging, and most of the talking. If you'd made the mistake of going eager beaver on him with a lot of suggestions, you wouldn't last long. When he does call you in to look at a treatment, see me. I can tell you what to do."

I bet she could, at that. Somehow, I'd never quite realized that Pat was a business woman, and a damned good one. Seeing her behind the desk, handling the office, reminded me. She looked competent. And elegant. I wanted to muss her up a bit.

"You're looking good, pal."

"You too. But why the scarf?"

I touched my neck. "That flu attack—my throat still seems to bother me once in a while. Sensitive to drafts."

"Oh." It was a subject neither of us wanted to discuss very much. She began tapping her heel on the floor.

"How's Jeff?"

The tapping ceased. "Wonderful. He's down in San Berdoo now, hunting for an office. I think he'll begin practice with his father in a month or so."

"Then you'll be married."

"Uh-huh."

"I'm happy for you, Pat."

"You don't look very happy for a successful author."

"Personally speaking, I'm not. After all, I'm a stranger here myself. Don't know the town. Or anybody. Except you."

"You'll get around."

"I was wondering if you'd help me get started."

"How?"

"Dinner."

"There we go again," she sighed. "Persistent, aren't you?"

"My mother told me there'd be women like this," I said. "Seriously, Pat—won't you have dinner with me? *Just* dinner, if you like. After all, a little food never hurt anyone."

"If I know my vitamins, you have more than food on your mind."

"I'll be good. Come on—I'm lonesome."

"All right. But just this once."

"Where'll I meet you?"

"Pick me up right here at the office. Around five."

"Good."

I walked out. As I stood waiting for the elevator, I touched the scarf again and smiled.

"I knew you'd bring me luck," I said.

The little man in the green sports coat was leaning against the tobacco shop as I passed. He didn't even pretend to be reading the racing form, just held it extended before him and stared at me.

I walked around the corner and looked back. Sure enough, he was ambling along. He must have seen me, because he turned his head and squinted at a window display.

I walked quickly down the block and crossed Wilshire with the lights. In front of the hotel I paused. He was going down the street on the other side.

On Canon Drive I slowed down again until I saw him shuffle over and head my way. Then I made double time.

I ducked through the yard next door to my bungalow and went in the back way. I locked the kitchen door and headed right for the front room. Pulling back the curtain, I peered through the glass at the street before the house.

There was nobody in sight. Nobody at all.

XIX

It was very late. The little cocktail lounge was dark. The leather surface of the booth squeaked as I moved closer to Pat.

"Why don't you marry me?" I asked.

"Jeff," she said.

I tilted her head back and her hat fell off. Her face, white and waiting, loomed large. Her lips were soft.

"You've got to marry me."

"Jeff."

She yielded limply. That is, her lips and shoulders and arms yielded. But she whispered again, "Jeff."

To hell with that, it was only a name, what's in a name. I had her lips and she was close to me. Wasn't that enough?

And then, out of the corner of my eye, I saw the coat, draped over the top of our booth. Just a green sports coat.

I sat up.

"What's the matter?"

"Late. Let's get out of here."

"I'm sorry, Dan. You know that."

"It's all right."

"But I am sorry."

"I said it's all right. Let's get out of here."

I stood up. As I did so, the coat slid down over the back of the booth. Pat put her hat on and I helped her around the side of the table. She headed for the door and I paid the waiter. Then I followed her, glancing into the booth back of ours.

It was empty. But a half-finished cigarette rested on the lip of an ash tray, and a gray spiral of smoke curved upward in a question mark.

The next night we sat in the fake cellar and drank the fake tequila and listened to the fake Mexicans singing.

"Why don't you take off that scarf?" she said. "You must be roasting."

"It doesn't bother me. Nothing bothers me, except you."

"Dan, you promised——"

"I didn't mean it, and you knew I didn't."

"Well, you've got to. I've seen you every night this week, but Jeff is coming back and then——"

"And then you're going to tell him you've changed your mind. That you love me."

She shook her head.

"I love Jeff."

"Seems to me I've heard that somewhere before," I said.

"Sooner or later you'll believe it."

"All right, just for the sake of argument, I do believe it. So let's consider the other side of the question. Does Jeff love you?"

"Of course he does."

It was my turn to shake my head.

"Jeff doesn't love anybody," I told her. "He can't. He's a psychoanalyst."

"Listen here, Dan Morley——"

"You're cute when you're angry. But you listen to me." I took her hand.

"I've talked to Jeff. I know him. And what's more important, I've talked to his wife."

She looked into her glass, but she didn't take her hand away.

"Jeff hated Constance. I suppose you know that. But do you know why?

"I'll tell you—it was because Constance loved him. That's why. And Jeff doesn't understand love. He talks a good game. He can analyze and rationalize and explain. He knows all the tags, all the names, all the labels.

"He hung some pretty labels on Constance. Oh, why pretend—he must have talked about her to you, too. Called her a nympholept, didn't he? A neurotic.

"But she wasn't, Pat. Take my word for it. Constance was just a sensitive woman who happened to fall in love with the wrong man. He analyzed her, prescribed for her, treated her—did everything except the one thing she wanted and needed above all else. He didn't *love* her. Bitterness drove her to divorce. When you and Jeff got together, she took me on the rebound, still hoping to make him jealous. And when that failed, and she knew there was nothing left except to go ahead with the pretense and actually carry out her threat of marrying me—she killed herself."

"Dan!"

"Jeff wouldn't tell you that, would he? He has a different story, I suppose. A theory. A theory about Constance, and me, and suicide, and people who are accident-prone, and all the rest of it. I know. He'll spend an hour describing a fugue or a syndrome to you—but he won't admit the truth, even to himself."

"That's not fair, Dan. You know Jeff is good, and kind, and——"

"Of course he is. And if you married him, he'd make a wonderful husband. He'd protect you, guide you, help you. He'd do everything except love you."

"Jeff loves me. I know he does."

"He loves you as much as he is capable of loving a woman—the way a father loves his daughter. Jeff is paternal. Because basically, he has no real need for you or any woman."

Her hand was warm and moist in mine.

"Marry me, Pat. I don't know how much protection, how much guidance I can give you. I guess I'm a sort of a phony. But one thing is real—and you know it. I do need you. And I do love you. The way a man loves a woman. The way you want to be loved."

"No, Dan. You're wrong," Pat said.

But her fingers dug into my palm until the nails crucified the skin.

We went up to the bar of this flashy place on Western, and I ordered Martinis. A new day, a new drink.

"How's it going?" she said.

"Not too badly. I went over to Hague's place this morning and he showed me the treatment. I had to read it twice before I recognized anything of my book in it. The two writers he has, they even changed the ending so that she doesn't really kill her husband and the whole bathtub gimmick is out, of course."

"I told you what to expect."

We touched glasses and drank. "Yes. And thanks for the advice you handed out, too. He kept watching me all the while I was reading, waiting for my reaction. I never batted an eye. The two writers were itching for me to start something, I could see that—particularly the gal.

"So I told him the whole deal was wonderful, except for one thing—he killed the ending by taking out the bathtub gimmick.

"It was just the way you said it would be. All three of them jumped down my throat, about how you couldn't work such a thing in pictures, and the fact that she wasn't really a murderess was enough of a punch.

"Then I let them have it, about two punches being better than one, and if they took the bathtub gimmick out they should substitute something else—that would work. Hague perked up his ears and asked what did I have in mind.

"I came out with that idea I told you about the other day: where he tries to frighten her into the belief that she really is a murderess by planting the body of the detective he killed in her closet.

"The gal writer took it from there, and suggested a dream sequence—he drugs her before he shows her the body—the whole thing worked out like a nightmare.

"That was nice, because it meant I had the writers on my side, too. So when we left, Hague was getting another treatment from them, and I guess I'm in."

"What do you mean?"

I grinned. "He said he liked the way I talked the idea. And maybe it would be best if I did have a finger in the final script at that. Dialogue. Six more weeks at double the money, plus a guarantee of screen credit. He'll call you tomorrow about the details."

"Dan—I'm so happy."

"Me too."

But I wasn't.

I saw him coming through the door, still wearing the green sports coat. He kind of stiffened when he caught sight of me in the bar mirror, and changed his mind about sitting down next to us. I watched him move along toward the rear of the place, the coat sagging from his puny shoulders. The wrinkled back moved up and down in quick darting ripples, like the green skin of a lizard.

"Pardon me," I said to Pat, standing up.

"Well, this is an unexpected pleasure. Don't bother to get up, old man."

I wheeled.

Jeff Ruppert smiled at me.

"No, I didn't know, darling. When I called the office, they just said you were gone for the day. It's just a lucky accident, that's all."

I didn't think it was so lucky.

"Been showing Dan the town, eh?"

"A little. Actually, he was telling me what happened on his story conference this morning."

"That's right—you're working on your movie sale, aren't you?"

I nodded, glancing down the bar. The little man was sitting way off at the end, pretending to drink a cocktail.

Pat's voice recalled me, although she was talking to Jeff.

"But darling, you must tell me. Did you get it?"

"Sure thing. Dad and I signed a lease this morning. Nice suite, completely furnished. I'll run you down and let you take a look at it when we have time."

"What about right now?"

"Do you mean it?"

"Of course I do. I'm so happy."

To *him* she said it as if she meant it.

I looked away again. He was gulping the cocktail and his eyes rose over it like twin moons above a lake of fire.

"Dan, would you mind terribly if——"

"Sure," I said. "Sure, run along. I understand. I've got an appointment in a little while anyhow."

Somehow they left. Somehow I said good-by. Somehow I managed to hold back until they got out of the door before I started down the bar. I held on to my scarf very tightly, walking fast and stiff-legged.

He was gone.

For a moment I couldn't figure it out. Then I saw the door at the back and pushed it open.

He was standing in front of the washbasin all alone when I came in. He saw me in the mirror and bent his head.

I walked up. I hated to touch that green coat, but I grabbed the cloth at the back of the neck and swung him around. He dangled.

"All right, you," I said.

He made little squeaking lizard-noises in his throat. It pulsed up and down.

"Say, what's the big idea?" he squeaked.

"I'll ask the questions. You answer."

"Put me down before——"

I shook the rest of the sentence back down his gullet.

"Talk fast," I said. "How much did he pay you?"

"I don't know what you're talking about. I never saw you before in my life."

"Yes you did. Over in Beverly Hills last week. The other night, in a tavern. And here."

"Coincidence——"

"Yeah. Sure. The long arm of Coincidence. Well, I'm going to twist it."

I twisted his arm. He began to cry.

"Spit it out," I snarled. "Where else have you followed me? How much does Ruppert pay you—he is paying you, isn't he? You tipped him off that we were here, didn't you? Didn't you?"

He tried to claw at my arm. Bubbles formed on his lips.

"What are you trying to find out?" I yelled. "Is it about Pat? Or New York? Talk—you won't get another chance."

"Stop—you're crazy—help——"

I hit him with everything I had. When he slumped to the floor, the green sports coat wobbled and his shoulders heaved. He looked like a snake that had been run over by a truck.

Without turning around again, I walked out and marched up to the bar. I ordered a double shot and downed it.

"Hey, buddy," I said.

The bartender turned, poising the bottle expectantly.

"Not that," I told him. "But I think there's somebody sick in the john."

He came around the bar and followed me. I held the door open for him.

"What's the matter?"

"You better go home, mister. Ain't nobody in here."

I looked.

The place was empty, all right.

XX

I WAS beginning to notice things.

Some days, driving out Wilshire to the beach and Hague's house, I'd watch people swinging their arms as they walked.

Tall men, whirring like windmills. Little guys walking stiff, arms held in tight at the sides. Women holding a purse and making choppy motions with the free arm. Queers fluttering like birds with broken wings. People swimming through the air with a breast stroke. Walking corpses, with hands limp and dangling from dead wrists. I couldn't stop looking. . . .

Then there were times when I sat in bars, looking at people who smoked. Chain smokers, nervous smokers, affected smokers, angry smokers. Puffers. Suckers. Biters. Chewers. Everywhere I turned, I saw smokers. . . .

At Teffner's office, or Hague's house, I'd notice the telephone talkers—how their voices changed as they picked up the phone. Two-bit menials, suddenly brisk and confidently professional. Barking big shots modulating their voices to a cooing gush. Timid, softspoken men, making love to the mouthpiece. The world would be full of voices, all talking into little black holes. . . .

Everything looked funny to me, but it all made a strange sort of sense.

The way, some days, every second woman I passed was pregnant—as though they were all hit at the same time by the fragments of an exploding sperm bomb.

The days I missed out on my timing: the stoplight turned red just as I reached the intersection, the parking lot guy was suddenly full up, the elevator door closed the moment I walked toward it, the line was always busy. I was cut off from the world, completely cut off.

Maybe it came from not seeing Pat any more.

I stayed away from her office and just went out to Hague's beach house, working with his writers on the rough draft of a shooting script. But I missed her, terribly. And maybe that's why I noticed things.

Maybe it came from drinking a little too much and then wandering around the streets late at night, staring at the cats who own the world when we're asleep.

Maybe it came from wondering about that little guy in the green coat—the guy who disappeared so suddenly.

Sure. That was probably it. I kept noticing things because I was waiting to see the guy again. I kept waiting for him to show up. Not that I wanted to see him. I didn't. But I had to see him, now. Just to prove to myself that he was there, had been there, that there was such a man.

Because if I didn't run into him, how would I ever know that it wasn't all my imagination?

Sure, I knew what he looked like. I could remember every detail. Why, I'd talked to him, hadn't I? And he talked to me, and I held him by his throat, I felt it under my fingers, I had fixed his clock for him, hadn't I? Hadn't I?

Maybe I hadn't.

Pat never saw him, the bartender never saw him. Perhaps I never saw him. I couldn't analyze it. What did that face mean to me? What was the significance of a green sports coat? Might as well ask a d.t. victim the significance of a pink elephant. He sees them, but he doesn't understand.

Only this wasn't a pink elephant. Either the man was real, or he was a guilt fantasy of my own. Delusions of persecution, that's what I had. I was cracking up, in my world of little men, and people who swung their arms and smoked and whispered into telephones.

Maybe it all came from a guilty conscience. Was that the answer?

Or maybe it came from wearing the scarf.

I wore the scarf because of my throat. And because Hague had noticed it, and liked to make a gag when he saw it. And because it brought me good luck. And because it made me feel different.

It set me apart from the arm swingers, the smokers, the phoners.

I didn't have Pat. I didn't have anybody or anything that mattered a damn to me. But I did have the scarf. I was different. . . .

One day, out at Hague's, we started kicking the story around as usual when a man came in.

Hague stopped the work and we all went into the next room. I figured something unusual had come up because Hague even turned off his phonograph. Sure enough, once we had settled down in the other room, the stranger took over.

The man's name was Duke Kling.

He was a tall, thin, wrinkled-up guy with a dead white skin. I noticed that immediately, because out there everybody has a tan. But his skin was pale—pale and wrinkled.

Kling was a news photographer for one of the papers, and he was on hand to take a couple of flashes for Hague. Something to do with a premiere coming up the next week.

Hague introduced us afterwards.

"*Lucky Lady*," said Kling. "Sure. The bathtub murder. I read it. Isn't a murder book out I don't read."

"But it's not exactly a mystery," I said. "And it isn't actually out yet."

"Read the advance copy," Kling explained. "My girl friend gets 'em for me. She always does. Murders and accidents—that's my business."

His blinking, watery eyes never left my face.

"I'll bet I could give you some sweet ideas, son," he said. "You see a lot of things in my racket." He finished packing his stuff as I said so-long to the others.

"Going into town?" he asked. "How about giving me a lift?"

"Sure."

In the car, driving back, he kept talking and talking. I couldn't shake him, and it made me nervous.

"Let me buy you a drink," he insisted. "This is something right up my alley—I'd like to tell you a few things."

We pulled up at some joint and went inside.

He bought one and I bought one. All the while he asked questions about where I got my plots; if I'd ever run across my material in real life.

The more nervous I got, the more I drank. But I couldn't walk out on the guy. It would look too funny.

"You should have covered some of the assignments I've had," he said. "There's lots of things never get into the paper, you know. Hush stuff. And some of it's too bad to print. Get what I mean? Bad. Messy."

He nudged me, and blinked over his glass.

"It's hard to believe, the things that go on here. Back in Cleveland I saw some pretty raw stuff—remember a few years ago, those torso murders? I was on some of those cases. They called him the Mad Butcher. And he was, believe me! Have you ever thought of doing a book on a guy like that?"

I told him no, I'd never thought of it. And poured another drink.

"Why not? People like to read about it. Look at the way those true-detective magazines sell. Sex crimes. Blood. Everybody wants to know."

"Out of my line," I said.

"You're wrong. I read your book. You could do a swell job."

"Not interested."

"Ever hear about the ritual murders we had out here? The devil worshipers? They cut up a kid. . . ."

The next drink went down faster. I was groggy. He gulped his down and kept right on talking. And blinking. He had a soft, mushy voice.

I got up.

"What's the matter? Going somewhere?"

"I have a date," I lied. "Almost forgot."

"Downtown?"

"Yeah."

"Would you mind running me by my place? It's on Bixel—won't be out of your way much if you take Seventh."

"All right."

I could scarcely drive straight. He hunched over me and talked.

"You ought to do it. There's a great book, a lot of books, in some of the stuff I've found out. And you have just the right kind of style."

I parked where he told me. My head ached.

"Come on up for a minute," he said. "I want to show you something."

"What?"

"You'll see. I've never showed it to anyone before. But I know you'll be interested."

I had that feeling of strangeness again—the same feeling I got when I saw the little man in the green sports coat. I didn't want to go up to Kling's apartment. I didn't like Kling. But I had to know what it was all about.

I pulled the scarf tight around my neck as we entered the cold, drafty hall. We walked two flights.

He had a dirty little flat in the back. I scarcely looked at it, my head was aching so.

Turning on a lamp, he disappeared into the bedroom and came out with a black book that looked like an old-fashioned photo album.

He sat down next to me on the sofa and handed the book over.

"What's this?"

"Take a look. You'll see." His voice was husky. His eyelids batted up and down like a couple of moths against a pair of headlights.

I opened the book. It did contain photographs.

The first was a picture of a nude woman lying across a bed. There was nothing pornographic about it; the woman merely happened to be minus her head.

It was a good picture, remarkably clear. I could see the severed arteries in the neck. . . .

"Keep on going," Kling whispered. "There's a lot of them. All pictures I took. Pictures the papers wouldn't run. The kind they didn't dare print."

I fumbled at another page.

Something came into view, emerging from a tangle of wrapping paper stuffed into a garbage can. It was small, but recognizable. . . .

"I told you it would be good," he chuckled. "Let me tell you about that one. It happened out on Main Street——"

"Take it," I said, standing up.

"What's wrong, son?"

"I'm getting out of here."

"Say, listen—you don't have to get so huffy about it."

"Shut up," I said. "Shut up before I beat your brains out."

"All right, son." His voice was soft. But his eyes kept blinking at me, just as they'd blinked all the while I looked at his pictures. "All right. But you don't fool me any. I know. I watched you. You like it, don't you?"

"You dirty ghoul!" I said.

"I watched you," he tittered. "You like it, too. I can tell. I could tell the moment I set eyes on you, son. You know what it's like, don't you? Don't you?"

"Get your paws off me, or I'll——"

He cringed, but his bony shoulders shook with a sort of hysterical enjoyment.

"You aren't fooling anybody, son. I can tell. I know what you are——"

I slammed the door and lurched down the hall. But all the way I could hear him tittering.

It wasn't until I got downstairs that the thought struck me. Maybe he *could* tell.

Right after that the script started to go badly. There's no sense trying to explain the problem, but it all boiled down to one thing—the girl was wrong. Changing the ending knocked out my original character, based on Connie. We really needed a new heroine. Hague's writers worked up a story line and then it was my job to go over the characterization, rough in some dialogue. And the heroine didn't ring true.

Of course Pat might have helped. I thought of going to her, but I couldn't. Seeing her with Ruppert was too much.

I had to keep away.

So there was nothing else to do but work things out myself. I had to. I was aces up with Hague right now, and in order to keep that way it was up to me to deliver the goods.

I was working in fast company. His writers were shrewd: the gal talked on her feet and the guy would have been a big-timer if he knew enough to leave the women alone. As it was, they kept amazing me with quick switches and angles and overnight revisions.

That's the competition I was up against. And I had to work on the heroine.

I sat in my place and tore up paper. Nothing seemed to work. They wanted some damned simpering little sugar-puss—what the hell, I couldn't write about that kind of a woman. I couldn't create a character.

I was used to writing about real people. People like Rena, and Hazel, and Constance. They were tramps. A nice girl——

Pat.

The whole thing hit me like that.

The way she talked, the way she tapped her foot, the way she held her head when she powdered her nose, squinting off to one side like a cocky little sparrow——

Yes, I could write a character like Pat. All I had to do was remember, to think about her.

I got some more paper, sat down at the typewriter, and began to rough-draft some notes. Two days later, I had what I needed for my script.

Yes, I had what I needed for my script, but not quite. There were a few little touches, things I'd have to check up on. I couldn't fake them; details were important and everything had to jell.

I started to shave two days' growth of beard off my face and as I did so, I talked the problem over with the guy in the mirror.

"Simple. You can get the rest easily. Go around to the agency and see her. You can take her out again."

The guy in the mirror nodded. He was all for it.

"What if she won't marry you? You can still be friends, can't you? And if you got her drunk enough, I'll bet you could even make her.

"To hell with Ruppert. He doesn't have to know. Why don't you do it? You want her, don't you? And it solves everything."

Mirror-face nodded again. I could trust him to agree.

I talked to him very confidentially. "And then, by God, suppose there was some kind of trouble. There wouldn't be, but just suppose for a minute. You know how to handle trouble. You still wear that scarf, don't you? If she puts up a squawk, maybe you can fix it so that she wears the scarf for a while——"

The guy in the mirror double-crossed me. He had a look on his face I didn't like. Then it seemed like *he* was talking, to me.

"No. You couldn't do that. Not to Pat. Not to her!"

I answered. I had to answer.

"Oh, but I could. I know it. And if I see her, and I have to, I will. Sooner or later it will work out that way. I know it."

The guy in the mirror looked pale. He looked bad.

"Then there's no escape," he told me. "There's nothing else left for you to do."

I went away from him.

I walked back into the other room, picked up the script, and tore the pages into a thousand pieces.

XXI

RIGHT after that, things started piling up on me. I had troubles. Little troubles, but they made a big heap when I added them together.

I'd go into a restaurant and order a meal. Only I wasn't hungry by the time it arrived. Then it got so that I couldn't seem to order anything. I couldn't decide what I wanted.

Sometimes I spent fifteen minutes at the mirror, changing neckties. None of them seemed right for the suit, or the day, or the way I felt. I put them on and took them off, letting one slip to the floor as I reached for another. I'd stand there, finally, empty-handed, my shirt open, staring into the mirror while the ties writhed around my feet.

What did I need with a necktie, anyway? I wore my scarf.

Of course I couldn't work. The crumpled sheets around the base of my typing table looked like dirty balls of popcorn. Even wearing the scarf wouldn't help me when I tried to work on the script.

Most of the time I just sat around, wishing I could see Pat and not daring to do anything about her. All I had to do was walk five blocks. She was close to me, as close as the telephone, for that matter. I could talk to her, see her, put my arms around her——

But I couldn't. I mustn't, ever. So I sat there.

I was sitting there one afternoon, late, when the doorbell rang. It brought me to my feet like a punchdrunk fighter.

"Hello, Dan."

She stood there, smiling. And Ruppert was with her.

"May we come in?"

"Sure. Sit down. Pardon the mess—I've been working."

"I wondered about that. You haven't called, you know, and Hague phoned to report that you weren't coming around to his place any more. He's worried about the script."

"He's not the only one. That's why I'm hiding out—trying to get it down on paper."

"How's it going? You know, if you need any help. . . ."

I smiled. "Don't worry. Everything's under control. I was just going to call Hague tonight and let him know. But say, this is an occasion. Can I mix you a drink?"

Ruppert shrugged and Pat nodded. I went out to the kitchen and did things with bottles and glasses.

Ruppert followed me and leaned over my shoulder, casually observant.

"Nice place," he said. "Pat tells me you're really going places."

"I get the same report about you," I told him. "Suppose between a new practice and wedding plans you're pretty busy."

He nodded. "Right. Otherwise I'd have been over here before. I've been meaning to look you up for quite some time."

"Something on your mind?" I had to ask it, but I tried to keep my voice down.

"Well . . . yes. But it's rather a delicate matter, and perhaps this isn't the place to discuss it."

His pipe fumbling didn't fool me. I looked him in the eye.

"Let's have it."

From the way he avoided my gaze, I might have been the psychoanalyst.

"Dan, I don't quite know how to begin. Maybe you can help me out, maybe you even know what I'm about to say. Are there—are there any . . . questions . . . you've wanted to ask me?"

Yes, brother, there are plenty of questions. Plenty of them! Questions like who was that little man in the green sports coat I saw you with last night? . . . is it a sign of insanity when you can't choose a necktie? . . . why is it that when you're right up to it all the way and should want a woman the most your mind suddenly goes blank and all you can see is a figure in a green dress? (that's it, she wore a green dress, why haven't I remembered that before?) . . . and what's happening to me, what's going to become of me, how can I make the dreams go away? I had questions for him, but here was one psychoanalyst I must never ask about anything.

So I lifted my eyebrows. "What sort of questions do you mean, Jeff?"

He talked low, confining his voice to the space of the kitchen.

"About Constance."

He talked low, but the name seemed to roar up in my ears.

"I'm afraid I don't understand."

"You've never made any attempt at finding out about the disposition of her estate."

"Why should I? We weren't married."

"You were about to be married. She was buying a house for you in your name. Weren't you interested in finding out to whom she left her money? You knew she was a wealthy woman."

I sighed. It came naturally. "Connie's money never meant anything to me. You aren't implying that——"

"No, don't get me wrong, Dan. I know you weren't after her money. But aren't you even curious about what became of it?"

"It's a closed chapter," I said. "I want to leave it closed."

Jeff shook his head, slowly. "The chapter isn't quite closed.

For some reason—emotional dependency, perhaps—she left everything to me."

"I'm glad." And I *was* glad. For one cold moment I'd been worried. "You should have quite a nest egg. I know her cash was tied up in the firm with Hollis, but she left quite a bit of insurance."

"That's just it. The company won't pay off."

I handed him a drink. "Why not? There was an inquest, wasn't there, and a verdict?"

"Apparently that doesn't satisfy the investigators. They've managed to stall off a settlement all these months, and I've got a good hunch they mean to re-open the case."

I had another cold moment. This one lasted, even though I gulped my drink.

"That's what I wanted to see you about, Dan. I've been getting letters from the insurance people. They're interested in hearing your story."

"I have no story."

"But you weren't at the inquest. That seems to be the point bothering them. They have an office in Frisco, and would like to send a man down to talk to you. Routine stuff, and I think a plain statement from you would iron everything out. Are you willing to see the man?"

"The chapter's closed, Jeff. Sorry."

"Wait a minute. It isn't a question of money, or of a favor to me, for that matter. Haven't you stopped to consider how it might look to them—if they are suspicious—and you refuse to see them, talk to them?"

"Suspicious? What in hell do they suspect?"

My voice went up. That was a mistake, because it brought Pat into the room.

"What's going on out here?" she called. The smile froze on her face, dropped off. I didn't care. I stuck my jaw out at Ruppert.

"Come on," I said. "Quit stalling. What do they suspect, anyway?"

"I don't know."

"We talked about suicide, once. Remember? And you were positive it wasn't suicide. Did you know about the money, then? Was it the idea of getting the insurance that made you reject the suicide theory?"

"It wasn't suicide. No matter what they think, it couldn't have been suicide."

"Please, Jeff, there's no need to get excited," Pat said. Nobody paid any attention to her.

"Then stick to your guns and tell them that. You don't need me. They'll have to settle, it's the law, isn't it?"

"Dan—wait a minute. What makes you so positive that it's suicide they're worried about? Couldn't it be something else?"

"Murder?"

Pat said that. *She* had to say it, it had to come from *her.* I stared, and the room started to wobble.

Somewhere in the swirling, I saw Ruppert's head, nodding ever so slowly.

"That's why I came to you now, Dan. Because you may have to make a statement. I'm not sure they could force you to do it, legally, but there's nothing to prevent them from checking up. Checking up on you, where you were that afternoon when I called and——"

"Jeff, what are you saying?" Pat whispered.

I shook my head. The swirling stopped. My teeth were grinding.

"I'll tell you," I said. "He's saying I killed Constance, that's what he's saying. Because he hates me, he's always hated me, ever since he knew how I felt about you."

"Now wait a minute, Dan, I didn't say——"

"Get out of here!" I gave him a shove toward the door.

"Dan, stop it!" Pat tugged at my arm, and I wrenched free.

"You too—you're in on it, aren't you? He's got you sold, I can see that."

"No. I've never even dreamed of such a thing, you know that, Dan."

"Get out, the pair of you!" I shouted. "Get out, before I——"

They left. Ruppert flashed a glance my way, just a glance. Then their footsteps sounded outside the door, died away.

I stood there, breathing hard, for a long moment. Then I remembered Ruppert's glance. He wasn't looking at my face. He had looked at my hands.

I glanced down. Twisted between my fingers was the maroon scarf.

*

I had been drinking for two days, and I don't even know how I got into this joint. It was just outside of Palms, but I couldn't find the place again if you paid me. That's how high I was.

That's how high I was, or I'd never have picked up Verna. She was one of the hostesses; her voice was too shrill, her hair was too black, and her slacks were dirty.

But we got to talking and kidding around, and I bought her some drinks just so I wouldn't have to sit there any longer and twist the scarf and mumble to myself.

Then she asked me where was I going, and I said Tia Juana and how would she like to go along?

I don't know why I said Tia Juana, except that maybe she looked half-Mexican to me, and in the back of my mind was the idea of running away from everything. Really running away, this time.

I was tired of running away alone. Tired? Why kid myself—I was afraid. Afraid of the way the guy in the sports coat had looked at me, if he had looked at me. Afraid of the way Hague would look at me when I told him there was no script. Afraid of the way Pat and Ruppert would look at me if I had to see them again. And most of all, I was afraid of the way a special investigator might look at me when he started asking questions, writing things down on an official form. I was all washed up here.

She was a tramp, sure, but she laughed a lot and she thought I was cute, and a week end in Tia Juana wouldn't be so bad.

We fixed it up for me to take her home and get some clothes so we could get started and make Tia before midnight.

She must have been pretty high herself with what I'd been feeding her, because when she found out I was too drunk to drive she only laughed and took the wheel herself.

I passed out in back, and the next thing I knew we were somewhere past Laguna. She suggested we have some black coffee, so we drove into a parking lot between a hamburger stand and a tavern.

But when I saw the tavern I wanted another drink instead of coffee, so I went in there. I remember having a shot of vodka, and it sobered me up.

At least I was sober when we climbed back in the car. Sober

enough to take another look at her and wonder what in hell I was doing with such a bag. I took the wheel.

She kept laughing and nudging me, and planting mushy wet kisses on my ear, telling me she didn't know what I had that got her so because she wouldn't dream of doing a thing like this and she didn't know what had got into her.

It was cold, and she tucked the scarf around my neck, and then we drove on. Only I wasn't as sober as I thought, because all at once we were on the wrong road, winding back up the cliff instead of going along the ocean. It was dark, and she pressed close to me. Her breasts were flabby. She wore those cheap pendant earrings, the kind that jangle. Her mouth was always wet. I was beginning to hate her.

I went away someplace down inside myself, inside the liquor and the darkness—someplace where I couldn't feel her body any more, or hear her voice. I was way off alone again; not driving to Tia Juana, not running away from the job or the people or my own face in the mirror.

I got off there, inside my head, and tried to figure things out. What was happening to me, what was I doing, what was I getting into?

It only took a minute. We were still going up a cliff road. And nothing special seemed to happen inside me, nothing at all.

It was just that I suddenly realized why I had asked Verna to come with me, and I knew at the same time I couldn't possibly go through with it—I couldn't wait until we got to Tia Juana.

I couldn't wait.

So I snapped back into myself and told her we must be on the wrong road and we'd have to turn around. I stopped the car and pulled over on the shoulder next to the cliff.

Now I could feel the darkness again, and the loneliness too—but only for a minute, because she put her arms around me and began to blow into my ear.

I couldn't stand touching her. She was drunk, clammy and hot at the same time. She kissed me and opened her mouth.

Yet I couldn't complain. This was what I wanted. This was what I wanted, because now I could take my scarf off, and while she kissed me I could bring it up around her neck, around Rena's neck, and Hazel's neck, and Connie's neck, and Teffner and Hague and Kling, and the little guy—around Ruppert's neck, and Hollywood's neck, and the throat of the whole goddamned world and squeeze it out of them so they'd never look at me again and tell me that I was a murderer—just squeeze and feel it giving way because mine was the power and the glory forever and ever——

Then, somehow, it slipped free, and she was screaming, tearing the scarf from my hands. The car door was open, she was falling out, running down the road.

I couldn't seem to see straight, even when the light hit me. Somehow I realized that another car was coming down the road. Maybe they'd see her. Maybe they'd see me. Whatever happened, it was too late now. I couldn't catch her. I could only put the car in gear and drive like hell.

XXII

Somehow I got home. Somehow I got into bed. Somehow I managed to sleep for thirty-six hours.

They could have come for me then and I wouldn't have been able to do a thing.

But they didn't come for me. Nobody came.

The third day it was like waking up from a bad dream and finding the sun still shining, right on schedule. As a matter of fact, the sun was shining when I got up and made my breakfast. That and a bath and a shave helped a lot.

I sat down and had a cigarette. It tasted awful. And yet the mere fact that I was sitting there smoking it in my own bungalow was good enough for me.

Why was it working out like this?

Why hadn't Verna gone to the police? Was she dead? Had she been too drunk to remember my name—if I'd told her my right name? Was she afraid to do anything?

I didn't have any answers.

So far, it looked like a lucky break. Maybe it was. It had to be.

Because here I was, back again, faced with the same problems, the same situation.

And there was a new problem.

Now I knew, for certain, what was happening to myself. Every time I got into a jam, every time I ran away, there would be a woman. A woman and a scarf. . . .

The scarf! Verna had it. What could I do about that? I needed my scarf. How could I go on without it? The next time—but there wouldn't be any next time, there couldn't be. I'd been too lucky so far.

Lucky. *Lucky Lady*——

The doorbell rang.

I was all right again, all rested up. I felt fine. But it took me three minutes to walk the ten feet over to that door.

Three minutes, while the doorbell rang and rang, and the police waited, the investigator waited, Verna waited, the little guy in the coat and Kling and Lou King, everybody waited. Waited to grab me, waited to get me, waited to look at me and smile and say, "We know what you are, we know all about it, better come along now."

The ringing was frozen in air. My hand was frozen on the icy doorknob.

I opened the door.

It was Pat.

"Dan—you're all right!"

She was smiling. She had on a new gray suit. Her eyes were clear. I couldn't say anything.

"Where have you been? I've been looking everywhere—couldn't imagine what happened to you. Hague is really worried; he called up half a dozen times in the last two days. We phoned here and no answer, and I've stopped by every night after work—"

"It's no use, Pat. I'm through."

"Through?"

"Licked. I can't do that script job. I don't know how. I was ashamed to tell you before, but now I must. I've been drunk most of the week and then sleeping it off here, dead to the world."

"But Dan, why didn't you tell me? Why didn't you come to me, let me help you? That's my job."

"Your job?" I laughed. "Why is it your job to nurse a drunken writer who can't even run a bluff because he's not good enough? Not good enough to make the grade, not good enough for you."

"Dan."

"Oh, forget it! I told you to clear out, and I meant it. So why bother, it isn't worth bothering about."

"Dan—that wasn't the only reason I wanted to find you."

"Something else?" I stiffened. "Something wrong?"

She looked away.

"I don't think it's wrong, Dan. I wanted to find you—to tell you that I've broken with Jeff. Broken our engagement."

"But——"

"You were right about him, Dan. He does hate you. And he's jealous. Jealous enough to try and frame you. He even had you followed. That's why I left him, I'd always believed he was so honest, genuine, and then to find out that he was willing to torment you with a pack of lies——"

"What lies?"

"About that insurance business. The investigator. When I asked him, afterwards, he admitted it. There is no question about Connie's insurance, Dan. No investigator wants to see you. Jeff made it all up, because he has a crazy notion you did something to Connie, in the face of all the facts. He thought you'd break down and tell him so he made up the whole thing. He told me, and he thought it was clever, and I couldn't stand that. I couldn't stand remembering the look on your face when he accused you. Dan, how can I say it? I gave him back his ring and told him to go away, and here I am. . . ."

I can't put down the rest. I can't put down how it hit me, and how I almost cried, and the way she fit, snuggling there next to me. All I know is that she did fit, she belonged there, she was there at last, and everything was all right. For the first time since I can remember, everything was all right.

We had just finished lunch—I hadn't even known she could cook—when she came over to me and said, "Now about that script problem."

"Forget it, darling."

"We won't forget it. Things are going to be different now, remember? Hague explained it over the phone, and I guess I have the general idea pretty well in mind."

"No use," I said. "I had to tear it up. I can't seem to make convincing dialogue for a good gal."

"But you have, my dear! Don't you remember?"

"Huh?"

"*Queen of Hearts*, silly. Your heroine—Hedy."

"You mean that soap opera you didn't like?"

She made a face at me. "We're not talking about what I like, now. We're talking business. And I tell you, Hedy's your girl. Why you can practically paraphrase most of the dialogue and the business from the book. At least, it will serve as a good working model."

"Say, that doesn't sound too bad, come to think of it."

"We'll work together on it. What's your deadline? Never mind—I'll call Hague right now. We can stall him until Monday. You have all your notes and the preliminary treatments here, haven't you?"

"What about the office?"

"I'll come over evenings. Oh, Dan, I've been such a fool! I could have helped you so much, and you needed help."

"I know what I need right now."

She came over to me.

Monday afternoon I took what we had done to Sam Hague. He was all set to sound off, but I persuaded him to look at the stuff first, and after that I knew I was back in solid.

Tuesday we had a shirt-sleeve session with the two writers, and Wednesday they took it away for the shooting script. That finished my end of the job. But Hague was already talking about another assignment. Nothing definite, at least not right now; just that he'd like to sign me to a contract. He'd talk to Pat about it in a couple of days.

I broke the news to her that night at dinner. "So it looks as though I'm all fixed up. And with the book actually coming out next week, I shouldn't have to worry for a while. Seems to me I can afford getting married."

"That's a pretty serious step, young man. Don't you think you'd better talk it over with your agent?"

"You're my agent. What do you say?"

"Sounds like a good idea."

"Come here."

"With all these people?"

"Come on."

Going home in the car, we talked it over. She had a little apartment out on Vermont, but I figured we could manage in the bungalow until we saw how things shaped up.

"Does Jeff know?" I asked. It was the first time I'd mentioned his name.

She nodded. "He called me yesterday, and I told him."

"He didn't like it, did he?"

A sigh. "Poor Jeff! He sounded just like an indignant father. And the things he said about you before I hung up on him!"

I wanted to know what he said, but I had sense enough not to ask her. Now wasn't the time. After we were married. . . .

"Let's get married right away," I whispered.

"Next month?"

"Next month, hell. I mean tomorrow."

"But we can't, darling. I mean, the tests——"

"What about Mexico?"

"Don't be silly. I'm still your agent, aren't I? And we've got work to do. Your book comes out next week, and it's important to capitalize on it. Hague will see the wisdom of giving a party. You've never attended a Hollywood party all the time you've been out here—that's really something to see! Then I'm wondering about a few bookstore appearances, and, of course, the trade papers will be around for a tap. Oh, there's so much to do, and so little time!"

"That's why we're going to be married tomorrow."

"You're just impetuous." She smiled.

"Dammit, I am impetuous! Tomorrow's Friday. We have the week end. We could drive right down in the afternoon. Come back ready to go to work Monday morning. Come on, Pat. Better catch me before I change my mind."

Her smile was augmented by dimples. "I never thought I'd elope."

"Well, you're eloping."

Her head came down where it belonged.

"Yes, I guess I am."

XXIII

I HATE to wait. I've waited for too many things in my life, and most of them were unpleasant. Waiting for the Principal. Waiting for the doctor, the dentist. Waiting to be let out of quarantine. Waiting for the damned freight to get moving, waiting to be sprung, waiting for the check to come through, waiting for somebody to find out——

I hate waiting. I hated waiting for Pat, that next afternoon.

My grip was packed, ready. I checked and rechecked everything. I took out my wallet and looked at my bankbook. Thirty-two thousand eight hundred. Not bad. Not bad at all. What was eating me?

I'd come a long, long way. I'd earned everything I wanted. I had everything, now. Well, almost everything—and I'd have that, too, in just a little while. I could afford to wait.

She was late. I dialed the office. Both lines were busy. Could something have gone wrong?

No, that was silly. I'd just have to sweat it out. But there was nothing to do but read.

About a week ago, I'd picked up Ruppert's new book down the street. After that scene with him, I had no desire to read it. But there it was, over on the table, and I had to kill time.

I opened *The Assassin: A Study.* For one nasty moment the thought flitted through my mind—what if it's about me?

Stupid notion. It wasn't about me. It was about John Wilkes Booth. Booth, and Lincoln, and Mrs. Surratt. A psychoanalytical approach to the assassination in Ford's Theatre.

Ruppert was telling the story from an entirely new angle—as a drama in which most of the participants were insane. Or at least, victims of psychotic delusions.

Booth, the megalomaniac. Lincoln himself, suffering from

melancholia, cycloid, given to visions and dreams of impending death. Mrs. Surratt going mad under the black hood she wore during imprisonment—the black hood placed over her head at the orders of the fanatic Stanton, twisted in body and in mind.

Weak-minded little Davy Herold was analyzed, and brutish Atzerodt. Ruppert had done considerable research to substantiate his theories. He dealt with all the conspirators in turn: Paine, Weichmann, Arnold, O'Laughlin. Even such minor figures as Spangler, Rathbone, and Dr. Mudd came in for a share of scrutiny.

And through it all ran the dark thread of madness. The tangled thread enmeshing them all in its ironic strands. And it was ironic that Booth the megalomaniac should meet his death at the hands of the self-castrated religious maniac, Boston Corbett.

It was a study in insanity, ending with the brooding specter of Mrs. Lincoln, huddled in a darkened room after her release from the sanitarium, wearing her widow's weeds and wailing in mindless terror.

All assassins, all killers, all murderers, are insane. That was Ruppert's theory. Why had he suddenly done an about-face on his popular psychology book? Why had he become so interested in a study of assassination?

Yes, and why did I have to read such morbid nonsense at a time like this? Why——

The doorbell rang. I gave a start, glancing at my watch as I rose. It was almost six o'clock.

Pat stood in the hall, carrying an overnight bag.

"Where were you?"

"Sorry. The office was a madhouse! Besides, I tried to make party arrangements with Hague this afternoon. I thought in that way, maybe we'd be able to extend our week end until Tuesday."

That made up for everything. "Clever girl! Come on, let's go. I'm hungry, among other things."

We went out to the car, and I stashed the luggage on the rear window-ledge behind us. I was in a hurry.

I got a funny feeling as we headed south. Only a week before I'd taken this same route, aiming for the same destination, with another girl.

But I had the scarf then, and there was no scarf now. There would never be another scarf. I knew that. With Pat, I didn't need a scarf.

She was quiet, and a little nervous, the way a bride-to-be should be. After a while she looked at her watch and sighed.

"You hungry?" I asked.

She shook her head. "Well, I am," I told her. "Let's grab a bite along here."

We had dinner in Laguna. There were clouds out on the water. A storm was coming up.

Pat didn't eat much. She bit her lip and looked at her watch again.

"Dan, don't you think we ought to turn back? It looks like rain."

"The mail must go through."

"But it's getting late. I don't like to drive in the rain. I'm terrified of thunderstorms."

"With me to protect you? Come on."

"Couldn't we stop here, or in San Diego?"

I squeezed her hand. "Aren't getting cold feet, are you, darling?"

"No, but——"

"Come on. We'll make it."

The storm hit us north of San Diego. For a half hour she hadn't said a word, and I suddenly realized she wasn't kidding. She was deathly afraid of thunder and lightning; I could sense that now.

"Cheer up. We'll hit the border in an hour or so."

The lightning blazed in off the water and the rain came down like a tidal wave—solid and hard. The little gray coupé began to buck the road. Apparently putting on California license plates last month hadn't acclimated the car.

Then we skidded, and the wiper stuck. I could feel Pat trembling at my side.

"We'll stop here," I said. "Must be a tourist place or an auto court down the road."

There was. The sign said TOURIST CABINS.

I pulled in under the spotlights flooding the gravel yard. Ours was the only car in the place.

"Get a cabin," I yelled, over the thunder. "If it's O.K. with you."

Pat's face was white in the lightning-glare.

I fought my way to the door of the first cabin, the one in front marked OFFICE.

The little guy with the pipe didn't ask any questions. I laid down my five bucks and got a key.

"Right across the way," he said. "The lights are out, I guess. Storm always does that, and I didn't expect any customers on a night like this. I'll have 'em fixed for you right away."

The storm was really blowing when I got outside again. It was a job just getting back to the car. I reached it, soaked and panting.

"Come on," I said. "I'll hold your hand."

I waited as she reached for her grip on the ledge, opened it in the dark, and pulled out a trench coat and scarf to wear over her head. Then I bundled myself up and we ran for the cabin.

It was pitch-black inside. The lights weren't working yet. I fiddled with the switch for a minute, then gave it up.

"He'll fix the lights in a second," I told her. She didn't answer.

Lightning turned the windowpane into a square green flame. I could see her standing there, her eyes closed.

"Don't be afraid." I pulled the blind and moved close to her, put my arms around her. She was shivering.

There was only one thing to do. "You're all wet," I said, as if she didn't know. "You'll catch cold. Why not take off your things and hop into bed?"

"No. I couldn't."

"Don't be like that, Pat. We may have to stay here all night, the way things look."

"I couldn't, that's all."

"Wait a minute. Remember me? I'm the guy you're going to marry. It's all right."

"No, Dan. Please don't."

She pulled away.

"All right. But take off your clothes, anyway. Your coat and shoes. Let me help you."

"Don't touch me!"

The thunder was rumbling, but she didn't have to scream it that loud.

"What's the matter? What's come over you?"

"I don't know. The storm."

"To hell with the storm. We're together. This is our night."

I tried to kiss her. She moved away. It was like a game of blind man's buff there in the darkness, with the storm crashing all around.

"Don't!"

"I'll tell you what's the matter," I said. "You're afraid. Afraid of me." As I said it, I realized that it was true.

"You don't have to be afraid of me, Pat. You know that. I'd never harm you. Not you, Pat."

The rain hissed down. The wind was tearing at the roof. I heard another sound, and recognized it. Very softly, she was tugging at the doorknob.

"Here, what's the big idea?"

"I can't stand it. I've got to get out of here. Let me out!"

"Pat!"

I took her in my arms and she fought me—fought me in the blackness, clawing up at my face and panting. She reached out to rake me, and at that moment the lights went on.

I looked at her, and then I knew what was the matter. She had snatched it out of the grip in the car in the dark, by mistake. She had worn it running through the rain, and it was still on her head now. The scarf. The maroon scarf Verna had taken away from me.

She stopped struggling. Even when I grabbed her shoulders she didn't struggle. All she could do was stare; stare and tremble, while she read my face.

"So that's how it is," I said. "It was all a gag, wasn't it? About you and me, getting married, running off together—all a gag."

"No." She talked as if I were choking her. But I wasn't. "No. It wasn't a gag, Dan. Believe me. I didn't know anything, until today. Until that woman came to the office. Jeff was there. She told us—what had happened. That's why I was so late."

"How did she find you? Why did she go to you?" I shook her, not because I wanted to shake her, but because I couldn't stand the way she was looking at me.

"She knew your name and she had that scarf. She said she remembered your license number and checked on that. When you transferred to California plates last month you gave our office as your permanent address. That's what led her to us. She wanted money, of course——"

"Why didn't you call me? Why didn't you find out if it was true?"

"I wanted to, but Jeff said no. He said you'd run away. He needed time to locate the Peabodys. They're the couple who picked up Verna in their car. They saw you driving away. That's proof, Jeff said. Verna knew where they planned to go, and he phoned and traced them to Ensenada. Jeff drove down right away, and he's probably waiting for us with them at the border now."

"Let's get this straight," I said. "He was willing to take the risk of having you come along with me, anyway, in spite of what he . . . suspects?"

"He wasn't. He begged me not to come, to stall you off. But I insisted. I said it would be all right, nothing would happen on the way, and he'd meet us at the border. I told him this was the only thing to do in order to lull your suspicions. And besides, he needn't worry about me, because I had a gun."

My mouth hung open. "You told him that, and you have the nerve to repeat it to me, now? Do you know what this means, Pat?"

I pressed her back against the wall. "Where's the gun?" I said.

She turned her head away. "There is no gun, Dan. I lied to him about that. I didn't think I'd need a gun. I didn't think we'd even meet him at the border. You see, I just couldn't believe what he told me, in spite of all that woman said. That's why I stole the scarf. Jeff doesn't know I have it. He doesn't know what I planned."

I waited until she went on. Her voice was low, tense.

"I thought I could get you to turn back. Or stop in San Diego on the way. I was going to tell you everything there, and let you explain. I didn't mean to lead you into a trap, Dan, believe me! I would talk to you, and show you the scarf, and then you'd tell me it was all a mistake, and we could figure out a way of going on. But——"

"But we're here, instead," I finished for her.

"Yes. And I had to grab the scarf by mistake, and now I know. I knew it the minute you looked at me, when the lights went on."

"What do you know? Say it. I want to hear you say it."

"Why ask? Why don't you get it over with, what are you waiting for?"

"I can wait," I said. "I can wait all night. Until you tell me."

She blazed up. "All right, Dan. I'm not afraid any more. I believe Jeff, now. He's always suspected, ever since Constance. He talked to Lou King in New York months ago, and on the way out here he stopped in Chicago. He found out things about this other girl, Hazel, wasn't it? He told me all he suspected, but I didn't believe it. Because I loved you." She laughed, and the thunder echoed.

"But it's true, isn't it? About you, and the scarf? You used it, didn't you? You used it on Verna, on Hazel, on Constance, and now——"

I didn't wait for her to finish the sentence. I had her against the wall, and the ends of the scarf were looped around my wrists.

"One thing you must believe," I said, softly. "I've always loved you. I always will love you."

She closed her eyes but she did not flinch.

"You can't kill me, Dan. I know that. You can't kill me!"

I shook my head. Then I twisted the scarf.

It looped around her neck like a fat red snake, like a band of blood. I grabbed the ends, pulled them tight, praying I could make this quick, very quick, for her sake.

My hands wouldn't work.

They fell away. The scarf slid to the floor. Then I began to shake all over, I was sobbing, and I couldn't help myself. It was true.

I couldn't kill her.

XXIV

I WAS lying on the bed with my head in her lap when they came in. They didn't break the door down—it wasn't even locked. But

Ruppert had a gun, and he kept me covered until the caretaker and a big guy I took to be Peabody held my arms. Pat wanted to stay with me, but Ruppert made her leave with them. He gave the caretaker his orders.

"Take a lantern and stand out in the road. A patrol car should be here any minute. They're cruising now between San Diego and Laguna."

They went out and closed the door.

Ruppert stood there, holding the gun.

"Why don't you shoot me?" I said. "Go ahead. Tell them I tried to jump you."

"I don't know." Jeff shook his head. "I would have killed you if you had harmed Pat. When you didn't show up at the border. . . ."

"So you were there, waiting," I said. "How did you locate us?"

"The car has been spotted all the way," he told me. "I wouldn't trust Pat to go off with you without taking some precautions. I tipped off the police in L.A. and the highway patrols all along the route were alerted. When the storm broke, just after I hit the border and met the Peabodys, I began calling in. Your car was reported leaving Laguna around nine, and San Diego hadn't seen it. So you had to be somewhere along this road.

"Patrols are checking back on all the tourist camps, but I was too worried to wait. I drove like hell back here—spotted your coupé parked in the lot as we were going by."

The little caretaker stuck his head in.

"Patrol's outside now," he said.

"Good. Tell them to come along."

The caretaker closed the door again.

I lay back on the bed. My knees wouldn't work to keep me standing.

"Please, Jeff," I said. "Kill me. Don't wait for them. Give me a little break. The state will fix it so I die anyway."

"No they won't, Dan. Not after the testimony. You'll be placed in an institution."

"But I'm not——"

I stopped.

"All right," I said. "Maybe I am. Maybe if I had come to you, before, you could have helped. You knew, didn't you?"

"Yes," Jeff nodded. He reached down and picked the maroon scarf off the floor, folding it.

I couldn't take my eyes off the thing. Steps sounded on the gravel, the two troopers came into the room, they said something to Jeff. I paid no attention. I was looking at that scarf. . . .

One of the troopers came up to me and said something about let's get moving, but Jeff motioned him back. At least I guess he did. I stared at the scarf.

Jeff held it in front of me. "It's symbolically significant to you, isn't it? Almost a fetish?"

"Fetish? You name it. All I know is I've had to have it. Ever since I was a kid back in Horton High, I had to have it. Ever since——"

Lying on the bed, looking at the scarf, I spilled everything:

"I had this Miss Frazer for a teacher in Senior English, and she fell in love with me. . . ."

I droned through the whole sordid story.

When I'd finished, Jeff sat for a moment looking at the scarf. Then he smiled wanly.

"So your writing became catharsis. And the scarf was a symbol of death. You wrote about women to exorcise them—and completed the exorcism with the scarf."

"I couldn't help it. It's like having somebody else inside of you, taking over. Your hands are tied."

"Your hands were tied, Dan. Tied by the scarf."

I stared at it for a long time.

"Do one thing for me, Jeff. Burn it. Burn it now."

"Give it here," said one of the troopers. "It's evidence."

Jeff gave him the scarf. Then the other trooper raised me to my feet.

I looked at Jeff. I wondered if he knew I'd tried to kill Pat, there at the end. I wondered if he'd understand why I'd failed.

But it was no use. I couldn't tell him, I couldn't tell her, or anybody, the reason why I wasn't able to go through with it.

I couldn't tell him that there at the last moment, when I tried to tighten the scarf, I didn't see Pat any more.

I saw Miss Frazer. . . .

XXV

They brought me here, and I told them everything they wanted to know. I went over the whole story again: about Miss Frazer, about running away and living on the bum, and learning to write. But they were more interested in Rena and Hazel and Constance.

You'd think that would be enough, but it didn't satisfy them; they tried to dig out more murders from the early years, only there weren't any, of course. I couldn't get them to believe that part about hating women.

The papers haven't helped much, either, calling me "Bluebeard." I'll bet Teffner and Hollis like it, because the publicity will help sell more books. I don't know and I don't care; neither of them have come out to see me.

Pat hasn't come, either. Maybe that's just as well.

Now I'm waiting to be extradited. I don't know when I'll be sent back East—so far they've kept me here long enough for me to write this all out.

Ruppert hasn't been around to see me since that night. It's a good deal, because if he knew about me writing this, he'd figure things out. You see, I started to write this as a sort of supplementary confession, but it's turned out to be the story of my life. And Ruppert knows what happens when I write about living persons.

They die.

The sheriff is holding my maroon scarf as Exhibit A, so that's out.

But I'll find something. Maybe my shoestrings will work.

Something will have to work, and soon. They're not going to take me into court and turn the alienists loose on me. They're not going to put me away in a cell, under restraint, tie my arms behind my back and leave me there until I rot, staring at me and tapping their heads, whispering about me behind my back. Maybe I am crazy, but I'm still smart enough to die in my own way. Quickly. And soon.

Funny part of it is, I still don't *feel* like a murderer.

www.ingramcontent.com/pod-product-compliance
Ingram Content Group UK Ltd.
Pitfield, Milton Keynes, MK11 3LW, UK
UKHW040928050225
454710UK00004B/164